Contents

Using this guide

Why read this guide?

The purposes of this A-level Literature Guide are to enable you
to organise your thoughts and responses to the text, deepen your
understanding of key features and aspects and help you to address the
particular requirements of examination questions and coursework tasks
in order to obtain the best possible grade. It will also prove useful to
those of you writing a coursework piece on the text as it provides a
number of summaries, lists, analyses and references to help with the
content and construction of the assignment.

Note that teachers and examiners are seeking above all else evidence of
an *informed personal response to the text*. A guide such as this can help
you to understand the text, form your own opinions, and suggest areas
to think about, but it cannot replace your own ideas and responses as an
informed and autonomous reader.

Line references in this guide refer to the Cambridge University Press
edition of *The Pardoner's Prologue and Tale* (revised edition 1994),
edited by A. C. Spearing.

How to make the most of this guide

You may find it useful to read sections of this guide when you need
them, rather than reading it from start to finish. For example, you may
find it helpful to read the *Contexts* section before you start reading the
text, or to read the *Summaries and commentaries* section in conjunction
with the text — whether to back up your first reading of it at school or
college or to help you revise. The sections relating to the Assessment
Objectives will be especially useful in the weeks leading up to the exam.

PHILIP ALLAN
LITERATURE GUIDE
FOR A-LEVEL

FOR REFERENCE

Do Not Take From This Room

PwN

'S
TALE
R

N

Philip Allan Updates, an imprint of Hodder Education, an Hachette UK company, Market Place, Deddington, Oxfordshire OX15 0SE

Orders

Bookpoint Ltd, 130 Milton Park, Abingdon, Oxfordshire OX14 4SB

tel: 01235 827827

fax: 01235 400401

e-mail: education@bookpoint.co.uk

Lines are open 9.00 a.m.–5.00 p.m., Monday to Saturday, with a 24-hour message answering service. You can also order through the Philip Allan Updates website: www.philipallan.co.uk

ISBN 978-1-4441-2159-9

First printed 2011

Impression number 5 4 3 2

Year 2015 2014 2013 2012

Printed in Spain

Hachette UK's policy is to use papers that are natural, renewable and recyclable products and made from wood grown in sustainable forests. The logging and manufacturing processes are expected to conform to the environmental regulations of the country of origin.

Cover photo: © David Espin/Fotolia

Key elements

Look at the Context boxes to find interesting facts that are relevant to the text.

Context

Be exam-ready

Broaden your thinking about the text by answering the questions in the **Pause for thought** boxes. These help you to consider your own opinions in order to develop your skills of criticism and analysis.

Pause for *Thought*

Build critical skills

Taking it further boxes suggest poems, films, etc. that provide further background or illuminating parallels to the text.

Taking it *Further*

Where to find out more

Use the Task boxes to develop your understanding of the text and test your knowledge of it. Answers for some of the tasks are given online, and do not forget to look online for further self-tests on the text.

Task

Test yourself

A cross reference to a **Top Ten quotation**. See pages 90–93, where each quotation is accompanied by a commentary that shows why it is important.

Top ten *quotation*

Know your text

Don't forget to go online: **www.philipallan.co.uk/literatureguidesonline** where you can find masses of additional resources **free**, including interactive questions, podcasts, exam answers and a glossary.

Synopsis

The Pardoner, who is not named, is one of the 30 characters that Chaucer assembles at the Tabard Inn at Southwark, all going on a pilgrimage to the shrine of Thomas Becket at Canterbury. His character is introduced in 'The General Prologue' to *The Canterbury Tales*, where he is revealed to be a deceitful man. See the *Characters* section of this guide on pp. 32–35 for full details.

The Pardoner, from the fourteenth-century Ellesmere manuscript of *The Canterbury Tales*

The pilgrims agree to tell stories on their journey in order to pass the time. Chaucer never completed *The Canterbury Tales*, so we do not know exactly how the Pardoner's tale would have fitted into the overall plan, but his tale is preceded by a story told by a doctor.

There is then a bridging passage, 'The Introduction to the Pardoner's Tale', where the Host comments on the Physician's tale and asks the Pardoner to tell the next story, hoping for something merry to entertain the pilgrims. The Pardoner agrees, but insists that they stop at an inn so that he can have something to eat and drink first.

Before the Pardoner begins his story he explains, in 'The Pardoner's Prologue', the way that he normally preaches in churches. This prologue turns out to be an explanation of the tricks and strategies he uses in order to make money out of the gullible people to whom he speaks. He takes a verse from the Bible, 'the love of money is the root of all evil', and shows how he uses this theme to enrich himself. He admits the hypocrisy of this, but is boastful rather than ashamed of the fact that he is guilty of the vice against which he is preaching. He cares for nothing except money, he says, to the extent that he is willing to let 'children sterve for famine' as long as he is gaining wealth.

After this long prologue — at 134 lines, the second-longest personal introduction in *The Canterbury Tales* — the Pardoner finally begins his tale. This is about a group of young men in Flanders, who live a sinful life of gambling, gluttony and whoring.

He has hardly begun his tale, however, when he interrupts it with a lengthy homily — a further 178 lines — on a range of vices including drunkenness, gluttony, gambling and swearing. This has the effect of delaying yet further the telling of the tale itself, thereby enhancing the audience's anticipation of it. It is nearly 350 lines after the Host asked the Pardoner to tell a tale that the audience finally gets to hear it.

The tale itself is very short — a mere 227 lines — but it has been well worth waiting for, being a concise and sharp moral tale designed to exemplify the Pardoner's original theme that 'the love of money is the root of all evil'. The Pardoner focuses on three of the dissolute young men he described at the start. They are drinking in an inn when they hear that one of their fellows has died, slain by a 'privee theef' called Death. In their drunkenness the three young men swear an oath to kill Death and set off in search of him. They rapidly encounter a mysterious old man whom they abuse, asking why he has lived so long and why he is not yet dead. Despite their behaviour, the old man responds courteously and tells them that if they wish to find Death, they should go up a crooked path where they will discover Death beneath a tree.

The young men run up the path and find a huge pile of gold coins. They instantly forget their quest for Death, claim the treasure as their own and start to make plans to transport it back to their own homes. The youngest of them is sent off to town to buy wine and bread. While he is away the other two plot to murder him so that they can share the treasure between themselves. The youngest man, meanwhile, hatches his own plot, and returns bearing two poisoned bottles of wine, planning to murder his confederates. Inevitably, the elder two murder him and then drink the poisoned wine, so that all three succeed in their quest to find Death.

Summaries and commentaries

'The Pardoner's Prologue'

Apart from the Wife of Bath, the Pardoner is the only pilgrim to whom Chaucer grants an extended personal prologue. This point is worthy of consideration early on because it suggests the care with which Chaucer builds up the significance of the Pardoner within *The Canterbury Tales*. The character, who is vividly established in 'The General Prologue', is developed at length in the Pardoner's own description of himself in his prologue. By the time we get to his tale, the character of the narrator has been fully delineated.

The Pardoner's prologue is in the form of a confession, a *confessio* in Latin. This was a conventional literary form, in which a character reveals his true nature through self-confession. The immediate model for Chaucer's Pardoner seems to have been the character of Faux-Semblant (False Seeming) in the long French poem *Le Roman de la Rose*, part of which Chaucer translated into English. The unrealistic and formal nature of the *confessio* is contrasted with the naturalistic manner and speech of the Pardoner.

Additionally, the prologue introduces the characteristic medieval sermon form, which starts with a statement of the 'theme' in Latin, is amplified through citation of authorities and the use of an *exemplum* (example), and concludes with a recapitulation of the main point. In the Pardoner's case, the parts are spread between the prologue and his story of the three rioters, essentially giving 'The Pardoner's Prologue and Tale' an artistic unity. In his prologue, the Pardoner explains his preaching technique, and how he begins with the statement of the 'theme', *'Radix malorum est Cupiditas'* (line 48) — 'the love of money is the root of all evil'.

Top ten *quotation* ❭

Lines 1–42

The Host comments on the previous tale told by a doctor, 'The Physician's Tale'. He then calls upon the Pardoner to tell the pilgrims some 'mirthe or japes' (line 33).

Commentary: **These lines form the introduction to 'The Pardoner's Prologue and Tale', the linking section which Chaucer uses to** move the audience from one narrator to the next. The Host is the innkeeper from the Tabard Inn where the pilgrims met prior to their journey. He has joined the pilgrimage to act as master of ceremonies and to take charge of the pilgrims' storytelling 'game', in which they will while away the journey telling stories to one another. He is thus the most natural figure to link the stories, and often comments on them in his simple and direct fashion. The character of the Host and his importance is dealt with specifically in the *Characters* section, pp. 44–45 of this guide.

As a student you need to consider how the Host selects the next narrator, but more importantly, why Chaucer orders the tales as he does.

It is evident from 'The General Prologue' that the Pardoner is a grotesque figure. The Host presumably wishes to follow a sad tale with something cheerful from a man who rides along singing love songs with his friend the Summoner, and who is clearly a regular drinker. He specifically asks for 'som mirthe or japes right anon' (line 33).

Chaucer's purpose is uncertain, given the fragmentary nature of *The Canterbury Tales*, but the two tales seem to share a moral purpose, although they are delivered very differently. It can easily be argued, however, that Chaucer wishes to vary the tone of *The Canterbury Tales* by juxtaposing very different types of story and storyteller. It is worth noting that he defeats any expectation the audience may have of 'mirthe or japes', for the Pardoner's tale is a macabre one.

> you need to consider how the Host selects the next narrator

The Physician's Tale

'The Physician's Tale' is based on a classical story by Livy which was well known in the Middle Ages, being retold in the French *Le Roman de la Rose* and by Chaucer's friend John Gower in his *Confessio Amantis*. A Roman nobleman has a beautiful 14-year-old daughter named Virginia. A judge, Apius, sees her one day and lusts after her. He gets an accomplice to testify in court that Virginia is a runaway slave, and Apius orders her father to relinquish her. Her father returns home and tells Virginia that he must kill her in order to preserve her honour, which he does. Apius orders his execution for murder, but the witnesses rebel and depose Apius instead. The story is a pitiful one designed to arouse the sympathy of the audience for the tragedy of the innocent young girl.

Taking it
Further

Look at 'The Physician's Tale' in order to gain a sense of the immediate context in which 'The Pardoner's Tale' operates. This will also enable you to see how Chaucer's style and tone vary from story to story.

Lines 43–48

The Pardoner introduces himself and explains that when he preaches he always uses the same theme: 'Radix malorum est Cupiditas' (line 48).

Commentary: **The Pardoner immediately proclaims that he is a performer, 'I peyne me to han an hauteyn speche' (line 44), and clearly a boastful one at that:**

> And ringe it out as round as gooth a belle,
> For I kan al by rote that I telle.   (lines 45–46)

His character is thus immediately established in the minds of the audience, very like the Wife of Bath who starts her prologue in similarly assertive and self-confident manner. The two of them have a great deal in common in terms of personality.

It is not immediately apparent to the audience that the Pardoner's proclaimed preaching theme, 'Radix malorum est Cupiditas', will be the theme and focus of the whole prologue and tale. The Pardoner skilfully introduces the topic which will occupy him for the next 650 lines without being explicit, so the audience is not given the impression they are about to listen to a sermon. Chaucer, with even greater skill, mixes the elements of the sermon/tale of the rioters with the confessional form of the Pardoner's discourse. The irony that the cupidity theme applies equally to the Pardoner and to his characters will become clear as his confession continues.

Lines 49–54

He begins his sermons by showing his licence to preach, in order to protect himself: 'my body to warente' (line 52).

Commentary: **So far, there seems to be no suggestion that he is anything other than a legitimate pardoner, undertaking the Church's work, with the necessary legal and spiritual authority to do so. Even this early, however, doubts begin to creep in. The falsity of pardoners and the likelihood that official documents were faked was widely known in the fourteenth century, and is ruthlessly exposed by Chaucer in his portrait of the Pardoner in 'The General Prologue'. Additionally, the suggestion that the Pardoner needs to protect himself raises suspicions. Who, or what, is he protecting himself from? Perhaps he fears a challenge to his legality; perhaps he fears physical attack from the people whom he dupes.**

Top ten *quotation* ❯

Task 1

Compare this opening of 'The Pardoner's Prologue' to the opening of 'The Wife of Bath's Prologue'. Describe the characteristics of each speaker. What similarities and differences can you find?

Top ten *quotation* ❯

Context

Visualise the scene: the Pardoner is addressing a group of pilgrims who have stopped at an inn for refreshments. If you are good at drawing, you might like to depict this moment. The scene is identical to that in which a pardoner would normally address worshippers, whether in church or in the open air, and it is possible to overlay the two images mentally. A further image to add is that of Chaucer himself telling his tales at public gatherings.

Lines 55–60

The Pardoner explains how he then proceeds with his sermons, backed by the authority of popes and cardinals, and beginning with a few words in Latin to inspire his audience.

Commentary: **The Pardoner softens up his audience by using Latin, if only in the text of his theme. This makes him sound authoritative. His audience would associate a Latin speaker with a clergyman, someone wise whom they would obey. He reiterates the idea that he is licensed by the highest authorities in the Catholic Church, popes and cardinals. This is intended to establish his credentials and make him seem to be at the heart of the Church, although you should remember that he is not a cleric at all (something he would like his audience to forget). He is like a conman who starts by providing 'evidence' of his credentials, or a doorstep salesman who flashes an official-looking ID card to gain entrance and a favourable hearing.**

Chaucer reading to the court of Edward III, as painted by the Pre-Raphaelite artist Ford Madox Brown

Lines 61–65

The Pardoner's first tactic is to display holy relics: glass boxes full of pieces of clothing and bones.

Commentary: **The first part of his repertoire is the 'holy' relics he shows, but he already confesses to the pilgrims that these are fakes: 'Relikes been they, as wenen they echoon' (line 63). He clearly does not intend to maintain a pretence of honesty or legitimacy, and this is a fascinating part of the duality at the heart of the Pardoner. He is a conman, but so self-confident that he does not mind describing the nature of his trickery.**

Task 2

Assess the Pardoner at this point. He is simultaneously giving a vivid account of the methods he uses when he preaches and exposing the falsehood of all that he does. How might the pilgrims react to these revelations?

Lines 66–90

The Pardoner quotes the words he uses when preaching, setting out his claims for the miraculous powers of his relics. They have the power, he says, to cure diseases in animals, increase yields, and even heal human jealousy.

Commentary: **This is a difficult passage for a modern reader to appreciate fully because we need to understand the mindset of the**

Pardoner's — and Chaucer's — audience. Medieval people would have believed fully in the power and efficacy of relics. The very fact that Chaucer's pilgrims are on a journey to the shrine of St Thomas at Canterbury is sufficient evidence of the nature of their faith, a faith that survives today in pilgrimages to places such as Lourdes. The distinction that needs to be made is not between belief and disbelief, but between true and false claims.

Medieval people were well aware that pardoners and others made use of false relics, which would have no merit and no effect. They could therefore be credulous about the efficacy of sacred relics, and incredulous about the claims of corrupt pardoners, and Chaucer clearly intended the audience of *The Canterbury Tales* to make the distinction. This is particularly true of the claim about the relics curing jealousy, which is outrageous because it encourages sin. The Pardoner can stretch his case because he relies on the gullibility of his audiences, even the pilgrims to whom he is speaking. The final line of the section, 'So that he offre pens, or elles grotes' (line 90), seems like an afterthought, but is a reminder to us of the ironies that constantly underlie 'The Pardoner's Prologue': the Pardoner preaches that men should part with their money, but he is the one who accumulates it.

> Medieval people were well aware that pardoners and others made use of false relics

Lines 91–102

Continuing to quote himself, the Pardoner states that unrepentant sinners cannot benefit from his relics, but that he will 'assoille' others who make an offering.

Commentary: **The first part of this is the Pardoner's cynical disclaimer that a sinner will have no power to make a true offering, thus protecting himself against claims that his relics do not work. He can retort that their failure must be due to the sinful state of the person concerned. The claim that he can 'assoille' (absolve) people of their sins is more subtle and more sinister. Pardoners had no such power; only priests, ordained by God, had power to absolve sins. The Pardoner relies on his audience's lack of ecclesiastical knowledge and their willingness to overlook this point in their desire to buy the 'insurance' that he offers.**

Lines 103–08

This is open confession, and a boast. The Pardoner boasts about the amount of money he has gained — a hundred marks a year, a huge sum — through his false practices, 'this gaude' (line 103).

Commentary: **The Pardoner switches from reporting his sermons to addressing the pilgrims directly. He flatters them by drawing a distinction between them and the 'lewed people' (line 106) to whom he normally preaches, admitting that the latter can be fooled with 'an hundred false japes'. The technique is clear; like any salesman, he flatters his prospective purchasers by claiming that they are too smart to be deceived by tricks that will fool others. The Pardoner is, of course, trying to deceive the pilgrims precisely so that they too will eventually buy his wares.**

Lines 109–16

The Pardoner comments on his preaching technique, explaining how he uses gestures and his voice together to persuade his audience to part with its money.

Commentary: **We must imagine the Pardoner using exactly the same techniques with the pilgrims as he tells them he employs in his sermons. He gives them, and us, the immensely visual image of a dove sitting on a barn and stretching out its neck. He boasts of his own skill:**

> Mine handes and my tonge goon so yerne
> That it is joye to se my bisynesse.   **(lines 112–13)**

Meanwhile his confession deepens with the admission that he uses 'an hundred false japes moore' (line 108). The confession of his own greed is blatant now, with the ironic statement that although he preaches against avarice, his intention is 'to make hem free/To yeven hir pens, and namely unto me' (lines 115–16).

Lines 117–36

The Pardoner states that he preaches only for his own gain, and he does not care if the souls of his victims go to hell. He claims that preaching is often based on such false intentions, and he says that he frequently defames people who have offended him or his 'bretheren'.

Commentary: **At this point the malignant nature of the Pardoner is truly shown. In a Christian world where the salvation of the soul was the first priority, he is willing to condemn his listeners to eternal damnation provided that he gains money from them:**

> For myn entente is nat but for to winne,
> And nothing for correccioun of sinne.
> I rekke nevere, whan that they been beried,
> Though that hir soules goon a-blakeberied.   (lines 117–20)

Task 3

How far does modern advertising utilise the same kinds of claims and techniques that the Pardoner employs? Are modern people any less gullible than medieval ones?

❮ Top ten *quotation*

This is where the literary form of the *confessio* is most at odds with the naturalistic character of the writing; the Pardoner's self-awareness and willingness to confess his depravity seem unlikely. Chaucer offers a picture of literary hubris, the arrogance that courts disaster.

The Pardoner continues by focusing on those who have attacked him or his fellow pardoners — these people he will publicly defame. Again, he openly admits his hypocrisy and the depths of his malignancy, comparing himself to a venomous snake:

> Thus spitte I out my venym under hewe
> Of hoolinesse, to semen hooly and trewe.   (lines 135–36)

The snake image suggests that he is like Satan, who also used words deceitfully to tempt Adam and Eve. A modern audience might be reminded of Iago in *Othello*.

Lines 137–48

Nearing the end of his prologue, the Pardoner repeats the theme of his sermons, and again states that he only preaches for his own profit. He claims that he does have the power to make others turn away from sin, but that is not his primary purpose.

Commentary: **This section contains a powerful statement of the paradox of what the Pardoner does:**

> Thus kan I preche again that same vice
> Which that I use, and that is avarice.   (lines 141–42)

He is fully aware of the irony and the callousness of his behaviour, and is even dismissive of the good results that can come from his evil actions. This degree of self-awareness may be unrealistic, but Chaucer is making a profound point about the degree of evil represented by the Pardoner. It is hard to see how the point could be more dramatically communicated than through the form of the *confessio*. The Pardoner condemns himself readily, and takes pride in the depth of depravity to which he has sunk. The audience can vicariously experience the pleasure of the damned man charting his own damnation.

Lines 149–67

The Pardoner completes his account of his preaching by saying how he uses popular stories that ignorant people love. He says that he wants all

Top ten **quotation** ❯

Task 4

Compare these lines with the actions of the serpent in the Garden of Eden in the Book of Genesis (Chapter 3) from the Old Testament. Write notes on the religious parallel here, which reminds us that the Pardoner has a holy function that he is distorting.

Task 5

Much of the power of lines 141–42 comes from the use of the memorable rhyming couplet form. Make your own list of highly effective couplets from the text which you can use in your essays to demonstrate Chaucer's control of language and verse form.

the good things in life — money, food, wine and women — even if that means taking money from the poor.

Commentary: **The Pardoner freely confesses that there is no boundary to his desire for money and possessions, and no moral scruple that holds him back from their acquisition:**

> I wol have moneie, wolle, chese, and whete,
> Al were it yeven of the povereste page,
> Or of the povereste widwe in a village   (lines 162–64)

If he had not before, the Pardoner here becomes a loathsome creature, willing to take money from the very poorest people in society, and willing to admit that he does so. His dismissive attitude to the 'lewed people' (line 151) and his callousness towards the 'povereste page' (line 163) and 'povereste widwe' (line 164) mark him out as something monstrous.

Lines 168–76

The Pardoner now offers to begin his tale, being refreshed with beer. He claims that although he is a wicked man, he can yet tell a moral tale.

Commentary: **This section contains a further paradox to add to that in lines 141–42:**

> For though myself be a ful vicious man,
> A moral tale yet I yow telle kan   (lines 173–74)

❮ Top ten *quotation*

Once again, he fully understands the implications of what he is saying, and it is true that the tale he is about to tell has a strong moral message. The fascination of the Pardoner for many readers is how a man of such apparent insight and self-awareness can be so morally bankrupt. It is Chaucer's craft to make the revelations of this 'ful vicious man' seem somehow credible.

'The Pardoner's Tale'

The story that the Pardoner tells acts as an *exemplum*, that is, a moral example or story that exemplifies a theme. The Pardoner's theme, as stated in his prologue, is *'Radix malorum est Cupiditas'* (line 48) — 'the love of money is the root of all evil'. His story shows how 'Cupiditas' destroys the three rioters. It does not only do this, however. It links a number of sins together and binds them to the character of the young men, so that their avarice is seen as just one aspect of their overall

Task 6

Imagine you are the innkeeper of the inn where pilgrims stop and listen to the Pardoner tell his tale. You fall in conversation with Harry Bailly, the Host of the Tabard in Southwark, who is accompanying the pilgrims on the pilgrimage. Write the dialogue, with particular emphasis on your impressions of the Pardoner.

corruption and sinfulness. At the end of the story the Pardoner reverts to addressing the pilgrims directly.

Lines 177–96

The tale the Pardoner tells is set in Flanders and it concerns a group of young men who spend their time in dissolute behaviour, drinking, gambling and whoring.

Commentary: **Although he will later focus on the exploits of just three individuals, the Pardoner introduces the revellers in a general way as a 'compaignye' (line 177) of dissolute young men, guilty of numerous vices and several of the deadly sins. The point is that they are sinners and blasphemers: 'Oure blissed Lordes body they totere' (line 188).**

Although this may not seem too terrible to a modern reader, a medieval audience would have recognised this as being at the most dreadful end of the spectrum of sin. Nor do the young men repent: 'And ech of hem at otheres sinne lough' (line 190).

Already they deserve to be damned for the extent of their sins, which are terrible both in number and kind.

Before continuing with the story, the Pardoner introduces an apparent digression in lines 197–374. This has two functions. It has the dramatic purpose of delaying the story proper, which maintains tension and expectation. More importantly, it has the thematic function of enlarging on the nature of various kinds of sin, linking them all together in a picture of human depravity. This makes the ensuing story more hard-hitting, and impacts more fully on the Pardoner's audience — whom he will later ask for money.

Lines 197–262

The first sin the Pardoner addresses is gluttony. He describes the behaviour of those who drink or eat too much, and that such sin means spiritual ruin.

Commentary: **Gluttony was one of the seven deadly sins, which meant that a person guilty of it would face eternal damnation. In common with medieval practice, the Pardoner uses several examples to illustrate the point. Intriguingly (to modern minds) he suggests that Adam's fault was gluttony. This is understandable if it is remembered that in medieval minds all the sins were linked, and all contributed to the chief sin of pride. Adam's eating of the apple is seen as the willingness to put bodily satisfaction**

Task 7

The audience has already waited 200 lines for the Pardoner to start his story, which is now delayed for nearly 200 more. When it arrives, the tale of the rioters totals little more than 200 lines. How and why do you think Chaucer neatly compartmentalises the sections of the text into almost equal parts?

before spiritual well-being; the severity of this sin, which might appear relatively minor to a modern mind familiar with the idea of over-consumption, is spelt out strikingly at the end of this section:

> But certes, he that haunteth swiche delices
> Is deed, whil that he liveth in tho vices.   (lines 261–62)

❮ Top ten *quotation*

That is to say, physical dissolution will lead to spiritual death.

Lines 263–302

The Pardoner moves seamlessly from a denunciation of gluttony in general to deal with the issue of drunkenness in particular.

Commentary: **Again his condemnation is trenchant, and its impact depends on the vivid physical description of the drunkard: 'disfigured is thy face,/Sour is thy breeth' (lines 265–66). This, and the specific warning against a particular drink, 'the white wyn of Lepe' (line 277), makes the picture as instantly recognisable to a modern audience as to a medieval one. The consequences of drunkenness are also all-too familiar:**

> For dronkenesse is verray sepulture
> Of mannes wit and his discrecioun.   (lines 272–73)

The effect of the passage is to build an overall portrayal of drunkenness and its awfulness.

Lines 303–42

The Pardoner moves on to deal with gambling, using Classical examples to illustrate his points.

Commentary: **The technique here is rather different. Rather than focus on the activity itself, the Pardoner emphasises the spiritual consequences of gambling. As with gluttony, his condemnation may seem extreme:**

> Hasard is verray mooder of lesinges,
> And of deceite, and cursed forsweringes,
> Blaspheme of Crist, manslaughtre, and wast also
> Of catel and time   (lines 305–09)

The Pardoner continues to emphasise the idea that all behaviours are linked, and that indulging in one sin will inevitably mean succumbing to many, with blasphemy (and therefore damnation) the inevitable outcome. His choice of gambling here may seem arbitrary, but it is one of the vices that is identified at the beginning of the tale, and all the sins he describes — gluttony,

drunkenness, gambling, swearing — are specifically associated with the three rioters who will shortly become the focus of the story. As usual, specific *exempla* are used to illustrate the sin.

Pause for Thought ⏸

Is gambling seen as such a problem today? If not, what 'vice' might replace it in a modern version of 'The Pardoner's Tale'?

Lines 343–74

The last part of the digression is devoted to swearing, which takes the form of blasphemy, and the Pardoner's references are to the Bible in order to emphasise the importance of this section.

Commentary: **As stated above, blasphemy is seen as the most terrible of all behaviours, because it is a direct attack on God. The language is uncompromising:**

> Lo, rather he forbedeth swich swering
> Than homicide or many a cursed thing   (lines 357–58)

The Pardoner builds up this section to a declaration that links the sins together and suggests that murder is an inevitable outcome, as it will be in the story:

> This fruit cometh of the bicched bones two,
> Forswering, ire, falsnesse, homicide.   (lines 370–71)

Pause for Thought ⏸

As a modern reader, how do you react to this long digression so early in the story? Does it make you impatient for the Pardoner to continue with the tale? If so, why do you think Chaucer has constructed the story this way?

The anger (ire) mentioned in line 371 is another of the seven deadly sins, and will be immediately associated with the three rioters as they begin their quest 'al dronken in this rage' (line 419). At the end of his tale, the Pardoner too will give way to anger when the Host confronts him (line 671).

Lines 375–405

Abruptly, the Pardoner returns to his story, focusing on three of the group of revellers he described initially. They are, characteristically, drinking in an inn when they hear news of the death of a friend. They are told that the man has been slain by 'a privee theef', Death himself, and they are warned against him.

Commentary: **The Pardoner (and Chaucer) keeps the audience on its toes by his changes of pace and subject. He re-starts the story with a neat trick, making it seem that the audience is familiar with the protagonists who have not in fact been previously singled out from the gang of revellers at the beginning of his tale: 'Thise riotoures thre of whiche I telle' (line 375).**

This saves time and engages the audience instantly in the story. The fact that they are already drinking in the inn before dawn,

'Longe erst er prime' (line 376), is a link to the digression which spelt out the evils of drunkenness.

Hard against this, the Pardoner introduces the subject of death, first in the death of one of their fellows, and then in the sinister shape of Death itself, personified and given physical presence by the innkeeper and the servant:

> Ther cam a privee theef men clepeth Deeth,
> That in this contree al the peple sleeth   (line 389–90)

There is black humour here for the audience, which is about to be intensified.

Lines 406–24

The three rioters respond defiantly to the warnings against Death, and make an oath to 'bicomen otheres brother' (line 412) and to slay Death 'er it be night' (line 415).

Commentary: **The rioters' absurd oath to kill Death is based on the irony that they have interpreted literally what was meant metaphorically. Death does indeed slay all men, but they assume he is a physical creature who can be found and slain in turn. The audience laughs at this macabre and futile quest. It is introduced by the kind of blasphemy that the Pardoner has already identified as particularly hideous: 'Ye, Goddes armes!' (line 406). He emphasises the point:**

> And many a grisly ooth thanne han they sworn,
> And Cristes blessed body al torente   (lines 422–23)

The humour of the situation is thus darkened by the serious and mortal implications of the young men's blasphemy. The Pardoner ends the section with another portentous and darkly humorous line in which the word 'if' is crucial: 'Deeth shal be deed, if that they may him hente' (line 424). The power of the tale at this point lies in the audience's superior knowledge; it is already clear that the rioters' meeting with Death will mean their own deaths.

❮ Top ten *quotation*

Lines 425–52

Almost immediately after starting on their quest the rioters meet an old man, who greets them graciously. The young men abuse him because of his great age, but he answers them politely and says Death will not take him, although he is so old he wishes to die.

Task 8

Write 'The Old Man's Tale', in which the Old Man gives his own version of his encounter with the rioters. Do not try to imitate Chaucer's verse, but find a modern idiom that allows you to suggest something of the enigma and wisdom of the Old Man.

Commentary: **The story of the three rioters is told with remarkable economy. The rioters have hardly begun their quest when they encounter the mysterious old man, whose nature is deliberately left vague. The rioters are too blind to perceive anything other than his age, and although he greets them meekly they are instantly abusive, in accordance with the characteristics the Pardoner has created for them: 'Why livestow so longe in so greet age?' (line 433).**

The old man's memorable and resonant reply that he cannot find anybody 'That wolde chaunge his youthe for myn age' (line 438) should be sufficient rebuke, but the rioters are impervious. The Pardoner (and Chaucer) shows how the pride of the rioters means that their downfall is both inevitable and merited.

Lines 453–73

The old man continues to speak politely. He asks the rioters to behave courteously and let him go, but they remain abusive.

Commentary: **The old man specifically encourages the young men to respect his age, a familiar plea in any historical period! In typical medieval manner, he quotes the Bible in support of his case. The rioters, in their churlish fashion, abuse him and accuse him of being in league with Death:**

> For soothly thou art oon of his assent
> To sleen us yonge folk, thou false theef!   (lines 472–73)

They demand that he helps them to find Death, a powerful irony which is clear to the audience, and which provokes a response from the old man.

Lines 474–89

Top ten *quotation* ❯

The old man answers their question, explaining that they will find Death if they 'turne up this croked wey' (line 475), because he left Death under a tree, 'and there he wole abide' (line 477). The rioters rush off without a word, and find a huge pile of gold coins under the tree. This immediately makes them very happy.

Top ten *quotation* ❯

Commentary: **The old man's speech crackles with contempt disguised by meekness: '"Now, sires," quod he, "if that yow be so leef/To finde Deeth…"' (lines 474–75).**

In terms of the story this is intriguing, for the audience as well as the young men. What will they find? The fact that the old man

left Death there means that he is unaffected by whatever lies under the tree.

There is no drawn-out tension in this passage. In keeping with the general economy of the story, it is immediately revealed that the rioters discover a heap of gold. The irony of Death taking this form is not lost on the audience, although it completely escapes the young men themselves. The audience will also note the irony that an obsession with money leads directly to death, yet the Pardoner has confessed to exactly that kind of avarice.

Lines 490–519

'The worste' (line 490) of the rioters takes the lead, claiming that the treasure is theirs and that they will need to carry it away by night to avoid discovery. He immediately hatches a plan to send one of them away, leaving the other two to guard the treasure. The youngest of the rioters is selected.

Commentary: **Again the rioters are blind to what is happening:**

> This tresor hath Fortune unto us yiven,
> In mirthe and joliftee oure lyf to liven   (lines 493–94)

The 'tresor' will be a painful death, and it is not a result of luck, but of their own choices. There is dark irony in the fact that death is described as 'so fair a grace' (line 497), and in the greed with which the rioters claim that the coins are 'oure owene tresor' (line 504). The drawing of lots is presumably rigged in order to get the youngest rioter out of the way, so leaving his two seniors to plot against him.

Lines 520–50

The leading rioter explains that it would be better to split the gold between two rather than three. He persuades the other to help him to kill the third by stabbing him.

Commentary: **The most notable feature of this passage is the greed that inspires the rioters' behaviour. There is a huge sum of money in front of them, but they are unwilling to share it three ways. This is in line with the Pardoner's theme, *'Radix malorum est Cupiditas'* (line 48), and with his own avaricious nature. There are further ironies in the use of phrases like 'my sworen brother' (line 522) and 'my deere freend' (line 546). It is easy to believe that, had their plan worked, these two would soon have been plotting against each other.**

Task 9

Analyse the ambiguities in the old man's speech. When he says 'in that grove I lafte him' (line 476) does he mean he parted from Death there, or that he placed Death there for the rioters to find? In line 477, 'abide' can mean 'stay' or 'wait for' — does he mean that Death is lying in wait specifically for the rioters?

*Pause for **Thought***

How important is the audience's superior understanding here in increasing their enjoyment of the story, and their awareness of the ironies it contains?

❮ Top ten *quotation*

Lines 551–92

The youngest man, meanwhile, plans to kill the other two so that he can have sole possession of the treasure hoard. He buys poison from an apothecary, and places it in two bottles of wine for his fellows to drink.

Commentary: **It is inevitable in the nature of the story that the youngest man plots to kill the other two. The Pardoner makes explicit the fact that he (and they) deserve to die because of their sinfulness:**

> **For-why the feend foond him in swich livinge**
> **That he hadde leve him to sorwe bringe.**   (lines 561–62)

In line 582 the young man is referred to simply as 'This cursed man' — a murderer, like Cain. He intends 'nevere to repente' (line 564), a chilling phrase in a story told by a pardoner, whose work should be precisely to encourage sinners to repent.

Task 10

Technically, one of the three bottles of wine is clean and could be drunk safely. Why does the Pardoner specifically state of the chief rioter that 'it happed him, par cas' (line 599) to pick one of the poisoned ones?

Lines 593–602

The two rioters murder the third as they had planned. They then drink the poisoned wine and die themselves.

Commentary: **The finale of the tale is the briefest of all the sections, emphasising its inevitability. The Pardoner unceremoniously records the death of the rioters in ten stark lines, saying: 'What nedeth it to sermone of it moore?' (line 593).**

Lines 603–17

Following the end of his story, the Pardoner describes the hideous nature of the death suffered by the rioters, and exclaims against all the sins that they have committed.

Commentary: **Balanced against the terseness of the story's ending is the extended way the Pardoner dwells on the painful death caused by the poison, and finishes with a rhetorical flourish (lines 609–11) which reminds his audience of the list of sins that he enumerated at the start. This gives his story a satisfying sense of roundness and fulfilment.**

Lines 618–29

The Pardoner completes his sermon with an appeal to its audience, warning them against avarice and offering them his pardons. He offers to absolve them of their sins so that they can be assured of 'the blisse of hevene' (line 626).

Commentary: **There is an abrupt change of tone as the Pardoner appeals directly to the audience of his sermon. In the wake of his powerful story he is able to claim the power to grant absolution, provided that they offer him money. As usual, we need to be alert to the ironies here. The Pardoner specifically warns people against 'the sinne of avarice' (line 619), then lovingly lists the riches he hopes to acquire through his pardons: 'nobles or sterlinges, ...silver broches, spoones, ringes' (lines 621–22). He appeals particularly to women ('ye wives', line 624), presumably regarding them as more susceptible. The most disturbing aspect of all is his claim to be able to offer absolution, 'I yow assoille by myn heigh power' (line 627), because this spiritual function can only be performed by priests. The Pardoner here exemplifies one of the best-known clerical abuses: his pardons were meant only to be able to replace penance.**

Taking it ▶
Further ▶

It is essential that you understand the significance of the Pardoner's claim that he can offer absolution from sin. Refer to the section on Indulgences on pp. 25–26 of this guide, and research further on the internet if necessary.

Lines 629–54

The Pardoner now addresses the pilgrim audience, offering them his pardons and relics. He explains that they are lucky to have a 'suffisant pardoneer' (line 646) with them to offer this kind of 'seuretee' (line 651).

Commentary: **It comes as something of a shock to the modern reader, and presumably to Chaucer's audience, to be reminded in line 629 that they are not being addressed directly, but are hearing second-hand an example of the sermons the Pardoner preaches. Such has been the narrative skill that we forget this circumstance, and the Pardoner strikingly switches back to direct address in the middle of a line. The depth of his cunning (or self-deception) is revealed when he attempts to play the same trick on the pilgrims as he has used on those listening to his sermon. He relies on the force of his words and the tale he has told to carry him through and persuade the pilgrims to buy his pardons. He harps on their fears, as any skilful insurance salesman would do:**

Task 11

Analyse Chaucer's decision to switch the Pardoner's form of speech to direct address here. Outline precisely your response to the Pardoner at this stage; what impression of him does Chaucer want to give? Compare and contrast how the pilgrim audience might have responded to his tactics.

> Paraventure ther may fallen oon or two
> Doun of his hors, and breke his nekke atwo. (lines 649–50)

Chaucer's audience, and the modern reader, are left to wonder whether this brazen approach will succeed. The power of the Pardoner's theme, *'Radix malorum est Cupiditas'*, is now doubly striking as his avarice manifests itself.

❮ Top ten *quotation*

Lines 655–82

The Pardoner calls on the Host to be first to come forward, because he is 'moost envoluped in sinne' (line 656) and hence most in need of the Pardoner's services. The Host reacts violently and abusively, and the Pardoner is silenced. The Knight restores harmony by insisting that the Host and the Pardoner make up their quarrel.

Commentary: **It would seem that the Pardoner's choice of the Host is a masterstroke, because the Host is known to react with ready feeling and without intellect. The Host, by his profession, would also be a worldly man who might well be sinful. But Chaucer has a major twist to offer, and ends the tale with wild humour. The Host's scathing denunciation of the Pardoner silences him, and exposes all his cheap tricks as exactly that — cheap. The moral force of the Pardoner's story is not lessened, but rather increased by the awareness that the Pardoner is as likely to be damned as the rioters. The silencing of the Pardoner has Chaucer's customary ironic force. The most glib and facile speaker on the pilgrimage is overpowered by one of the least intellectual and unsophisticated talkers. The fact that the Pardoner is speechless because he is 'so wrooth' (line 671) merely adds the mortal sin of anger to the list of those of which he is guilty.**

There is an additional irony in the Pardoner's choice of the Host as the most gullible pilgrim. The Host is in charge of the storytelling 'game' that the pilgrims use to pass the time on the journey, and he has offered a free meal for the best story he hears on the pilgrimage. If the Pardoner had hoped to impress the Host and win the meal, he is rudely awakened here.

It is worth noting that the end of 'The Pardoner's Tale' is also the end of one of the sequences in the manuscripts. There is no indication of whose tale was meant to follow this one, and no conclusions can be drawn about Chaucer's intentions or scheme.

Chaucer…ends the tale with wild humour

Themes

Blasphemy

It is difficult for a modern reader to understand the importance of blasphemy as an aspect of 'The Pardoner's Prologue and Tale'. An expression like 'God's teeth' may seem frankly mild or inconsequential, and casual swearing is commonplace nowadays. Although the crime of blasphemy was only finally abolished in English law in 2008, it had been diminished to the status of common law since the seventeenth century.

Yet in the Middle Ages, blasphemy was one of the most appalling of all crimes. It was abhorrent because it entailed disrespect or disregard for God. Blasphemy means having an impious (literally *im*-pious, not pious and respectful) attitude to God, leading to irreverent utterances or actions. The importance of piety goes right back to God's commandment: 'Thou shalt not take the name of the Lord thy God in vain.'

It is in this context that blasphemy in *The Canterbury Tales* needs to be understood. Equally, it is necessary to distinguish between the casual utterance that even a normally respectful person might lapse into, and the kind of hardened impiety that is on display in 'The Pardoner's Prologue and Tale'.

The Host, for example, swears in the Introduction, 'by nailes and by blood!' (line 2), a reference to the nails with which Christ was crucified and the blood spilt in the process. In a strict sense this is clearly blasphemy, and the Pardoner is right to describe the Host as being 'envoluped in sinne' (line 656). Chaucer makes no attempt to assert that the Host is a particularly moral or virtuous man, and in this he is merely being realistic. Clearly, people swore in the Middle Ages as they do nowadays. However, the Host is just an innkeeper, not a servant of the Church; there is no malice in him and his oaths are casual, more a mannerism than a sign of ingrained irreverence. Chaucer intends us to understand that there are degrees of behaviour; the Host is a mild sinner, but the rioters and the Pardoner are in a different category altogether.

It is worth comparing how the Pardoner describes the swearing of the revellers at the start of his tale:

> **Hir othes been so grete and so dampnable**
> **That it is grisly for to heere hem swere.**

in the Middle Ages, blasphemy was one of the most appalling of all crimes

Research modern blasphemy laws, particularly in other countries where laws are stricter. Examine the controversy over Salman Rushdie's *The Satanic Verses* or the cartoons of Muhammad published by the Danish newspaper *Jyllands-Posten* in 2005. This will give you an insight into how blasphemy would have been viewed in medieval England.

Task 12

Create your own list of quotations demonstrating the blasphemous nature of the rioters and the Pardoner. As well as deepening your understanding of the text, this will form a useful resource for coursework or examination essays.

> **Oure blissed Lordes body they totere—**
> **Hem thoughte that Jewes rente him noght ynough**
>   **(lines 186–89)**

The Pardoner equates swearing with the literal tearing of Christ's body, comparable to his crucifixion. This seems extreme to modern eyes, but it reflects the common medieval view of the nature of blasphemy. He later develops this point further:

> **Lo, rather he forbedeth swich swering**
> **Than homicide or many a cursed thing**   **(lines 357–58)**

This is even more stark. Blasphemy is worse than homicide because it is God who is being 'killed' by such oaths.

The rioters as blasphemers

The Pardoner (and Chaucer) makes the three rioters wholly sinful in order to emphasise how appalling blasphemy is.

The rioters swear freely, both to one another and to the old man — for example, in lines 406, 415, 464, 466 and 471. These are gratuitous blasphemous utterances, and the Pardoner confirms the depths of their depravity:

> **And many a grisly ooth thanne han they sworn,**
> **And Cristes blessed body al torente**   **(lines 422–23)**

The Pardoner ensures that all aspects of their behaviour are sinful, and thereby blasphemous. They are drunk before dawn (lines 375–77), they swear false oaths of loyalty and brotherhood (lines 416–17), they abuse the old man as soon as they meet him (lines 430–33), they are consumed with greed (lines 486–89) and they conspire against and kill one another (lines 594–602). At no point do they manifest any pious Christian attitudes or behaviour.

The Pardoner as a blasphemer

The depth of Chaucer's art is clear from the way in which he makes the Pardoner, who presents such a stark portrayal of blasphemy through the rioters, as guilty as they are. True, the Pardoner deliberately avoids verbal blasphemy in both his prologue and his tale. Clearly, he is conscious of his position and knows that too many oaths will alienate his audience. He swears only when he is off guard, speaking to the pilgrims at the inn before he tells his tale. He picks up the Host's oath 'by Seint Ronyon!' (line 34) and adds his own 'By God' (line 171). The fact that he swears at all is inappropriate, given his vocation.

However, it is in his behaviour that the Pardoner is utterly impious. Like the rioters, he wants to start off by being gluttonous (lines 35–36) when he should be reflecting in a devout manner about what he is going to say. He is careless about others' salvation (lines 117–20), and even about his own (lines 141–42). He freely admits the fraudulence of his relics (line 63), and worst of all he usurps the power of a priest by claiming to have the power to absolve people of their sins (line 627). His flagrant attempt to dupe the Host shows his contempt both for other people and for the God whom he is supposed to serve. He is guilty of hubris — inviting God's wrath by ignoring the consequences of his own actions. This disdain towards God and total impiety represents blasphemy of the highest order.

The Pardoner and the Church

There are two aspects to the Pardoner's work — the sale of indulgences, and the sale or use of holy relics.

Indulgences

Pardoners were licensed operatives employed by the Church to dispense indulgences. It is essential to be clear about how this system operated.

A Christian who committed sin, especially a mortal sin such as gluttony, needed to confess his sin to a priest in order to receive absolution. If he died before this spiritual cleansing took place, his soul would be eternally damned. Genuine repentance was necessary, whereupon a priest could grant absolution on Christ's behalf and as it were wipe the slate clean. In order to signify that the sinner was truly repentant, he would normally undertake penance, commonly dictated by the priest. A simple sin might merely require the saying of some prayers as a penance, but penances could be considerable. Pilgrimages, for example, were sometimes undertaken as a form of penance, and could entail enormous inconvenience and expense.

The situation became complicated, however, when the medieval Church developed the concept of a 'treasury of grace'. The theory was that the lives of all the saints, together with God's goodness, had created a vast store of spiritual wealth that was sufficient to counterbalance all the sins that could ever be committed by ordinary people — a kind of spiritual bank account. Sinners could gain access to this treasury of grace by being truly repentant for their sins, and making an offering to show their desire for forgiveness. The practice grew of allowing people to commute the penance required after confession, frequently by means

the medieval Church developed the concept of a 'treasury of grace'

of a payment. Pardoners were employed to provide indulgences, issued by a bishop or even by the pope, remitting part or all of the imposed penance. These rapidly grew in popularity, but were open to abuse. A pardoner might offer forged indulgences. In more sinister fashion, people began to view indulgences as pardons for the sin rather than a remission of the penance, and corrupt pardoners were happy for this confusion to exist. Chaucer's Pardoner actually claims to be able to offer absolution, instead of merely offering indulgences, thereby usurping the authority and function of a priest. As pardoners were laymen, not members of the clergy, this was a gross transgression of their role and had no legitimate basis.

Corrupt practices were known and condemned from an early stage. By the fourteenth century, the malpractices described by Chaucer were commonplace, and widely condemned. Chaucer's contemporary William Langland offers a close parallel to 'The Pardoner's Prologue':

> **There preched a pardonere as he a prest were,**
> **Broughte forth a bulle with bishopes seles,**
> **And seide that hymself mighte assoilen hem alle**
> **Of falshed of fastyng of vowes ybroken.**
> **Lewed men leved hym wel and lyked his wordes…**
> **Thus they geven here golde glotones to kepe.**
>
> **(*Piers Plowman*, B Text Prologue, lines 68–72, 76)**

> *There preached a pardoner as if he were a priest;*
> *He brought out a licence with a bishop's seals,*
> *And claimed that he could absolve them all*
> *For failing in fasting or breaking vows.*
> *Ignorant people believed him well and liked his words…*
> *Thus they give their gold to gluttons.*

Eventually, anger against the false use of indulgences was a significant impetus for the Reformation in the sixteenth century.

Relics

The importance of relics in the medieval Catholic Church depends upon the basic Christian doctrine of the separation of the body and the soul. Sinful men could not plead directly to God because they were unworthy; they therefore needed to approach God by way of an intermediary. The Catholic priest performed this function, but there also existed all the saints — the pure and uncorrupted figures from the Church's history who had died without sin and therefore had privileged places next to God in heaven. A sinful person on Earth could invoke the assistance of a saint, hoping that they would intercede to God on the sinner's behalf. Although the souls of the saints were in heaven, they had left their mortal bodies when they died, and so the bones of saints were highly venerated as relics of particular power. It was for this reason that saints' tombs — such as that of Saint Thomas Becket in Canterbury Cathedral — became major pilgrimage sites. Every Catholic altar contained the relics of a saint. Additionally, clothing or items that a saint had owned or touched would have holy attributes. Christ had been resurrected and ascended bodily to heaven, but some of his blood had been spilt when he was nailed to the cross, and the monastery of Hailes in Gloucestershire became widely famed for possessing a phial said to contain some of Christ's blood, a fact that Chaucer refers to in 'The Pardoner's Tale', line 366. The Pardoner himself claims to have a 'vernicle', a reproduction of the handkerchief with which Saint Veronica was supposed to have wiped Jesus's brow.

It is easy to see how such beliefs were open to abuse. An unscrupulous person could put forward any item and claim it as a holy relic. The Pardoner does exactly this, and confesses it openly to the pilgrims:

> **Thanne shewe I forth my longe cristal stones,**
> **Ycrammed ful of cloutes and of bones,—**
> **Relikes been they, as wenen they echoon.**
> ('The Pardoner's Prologue', lines 61–63)

'The General Prologue' has already made clear the falseness of the Pardoner's relics, for example the pillow-case that he says is the Virgin Mary's veil, and the pigs' bones he displays in a glass case.

There is ample evidence that all the abuses Chaucer attributes to the Pardoner were known to be commonplace in fourteenth-century England. For example, the contemporary *Fasciculus Morum*, a fourteenth-century handbook for preachers, refers to false pardoners who used animal bones instead of real relics. The *Memoriale Presbiterorum*, another fourteenth-century handbook for the guidance of clergy, contains specific comments about exactly the false claims that the Pardoner makes. Everything that Chaucer writes would have been instantly recognisable to his audience.

Gothic and macabre elements

One of the most noticeable aspects of 'The Pardoner's Prologue and Tale' is its preoccupation with death, both in the tale of the rioters and in the context of the vocation of the Pardoner, who offers a kind of insurance

Taking it
Further

Find other examples of famous relics in medieval Europe, such as the fragment of the True Cross at Santo Toribio in Spain. This will give you a good sense of the importance of such relics in people's belief systems, and you will also discover some outlandish claims. You should consider the credulity given to such relics, and why medieval people would wish to believe in them.

to people against the mortal consequence of their sins. For this reason, the text has been described as 'Gothic'.

This term 'Gothic' sits awkwardly in a discussion of Chaucer. It was invented to describe the genre of eighteenth- and nineteenth-century novels that were set in the Middle Ages (the Gothic period of art and architecture). These featured an obsession with the supernatural and macabre, with death in relation to these, and frequently the depiction of an unhealthy or abnormal psychological state. It is therefore a historical term, dependent on a backward-looking view of the Middle Ages, rather than one that can be applied directly to medieval literature. It is easy, however, to see how the term can be retrospectively applied to elements of 'The Pardoner's Tale', which shows the kind of obsessions that Gothic writers emphasised.

The word 'macabre' literally means 'gruesome', particularly in the sense of being associated with death. The word comes from the French *Danse Macabre*, the 'Dance of Death', which was a common subject in medieval art and literature. The word has particular relevance to 'The Pardoner's Tale', which has death as a recurrent theme.

The macabre

The emphasis on death is clear throughout. Centrally there is the rioters' quest for Death, which ends with their grisly demise at one another's hands. Framing the whole of 'The Pardoner's Prologue and Tale' there is the Pardoner's reminder that all the pilgrims are only a step away from death at any moment:

> **Paraventure ther may fallen oon or two**
> **Doun of his hors, and breke his nekke atwo. (lines 649–50)**

For a medieval person to die in a state of mortal sin would mean eternal damnation of the soul. In this context, the Pardoner's preaching and his story are meant to be disquieting and disturbing, making his audiences feel more vulnerable and therefore more likely to purchase his services. Every sin dwelt on by the Pardoner or committed by the rioters is intended to emphasise the importance of seeking salvation by any means rather than going to hell. The willingness of the Pardoner to let such damnation happen is deeply repulsive:

Top ten *quotation* ❯

> **I rekke nevere, whan that they been beried,**
> **Though that hir soules goon a-blakeberied.   (lines 119–20)**

The audience's awareness of the Pardoner's own damned state adds a further macabre element to these lines, and to the tone of the whole work.

Task **13**

You should establish your own clear understanding of the terms 'Gothic' and 'macabre' before working on this section.

The emphasis on bodily corruption

This aspect of the macabre resonates throughout 'The Pardoner's Prologue and Tale'. The link between the revellers' abuse of their own bodies and their 'tearing' of Christ's body through blasphemy is very strong. Medieval Christianity emphasised the distinction between the body and the soul, and the purpose of Christian living was to purify the soul for eternal life. The revellers gorge themselves with meat and drink, which the Pardoner terms 'cursed superfluitee' (line 242). The image that when a man is drunk 'of his throte he maketh his privee' (line 241) is deliberately disgusting.

The long description of the cooks' endeavours to make gluttony pleasant and easy (lines 252–60) is linked to the hideous description of the stomach as 'Fulfilled of dong and of corrupcioun' (line 249). The rioters start drunk (line 377) and end up dying from poisoned drink (lines 599–602). It is impossible to forget that the Pardoner has demanded food and drink himself before he begins his tale. In this context, the attribution of Adam's fall to gluttony (lines 219–21) seems justifiable, because through eating the forbidden fruit his body becomes corrupted.

The references to tearing Christ's body have already been mentioned (e.g. lines 188–89), but there are other aspects of bodily corruption. The old man is described as wasting away (line 446), and crucially the Pardoner himself is described as possibly a eunuch in 'The General Prologue'. Even so, the Host offers to castrate him at the end of the tale, as a final thematic reminder of the deformed state of corrupted bodies and souls.

The supernatural

To a modern audience, the whole of 'The Pardoner's Prologue and Tale' can seem to be imbued with the supernatural, in the form of the relics and promises that the Pardoner makes. However, a medieval audience would have taken these as spiritual matters, rather than supernatural in the modern sense. The truly supernatural figure in 'The Pardoner's Tale' is the old man whom the rioters meet. However he is interpreted, he seems to have more than natural qualities. He explains that although he wishes to die, he cannot. In a more sinister fashion, he claims to know Death, and to have left him shortly before he encounters the rioters. He is able to direct them towards Death:

> **For in that grove I lafte him, by my fey**   (line 476)

❮ Top ten *quotation*

Task **14**

Make a list of all the quotations that describe bodily corruption and decay in 'The Pardoner's Prologue and Tale'. This will give you a clear sense of the tone of the whole work.

The personification of Death

Death taking the pope and the emperor, from a fifteenth-century Latin edition of 'The Dance of Death'

The personification of Death in the tale is at once comic and disturbing. The introduction of him by the servant as an apparently real person is darkly humorous:

> **Ther cam a privee theef men clepeth Deeth,**
> **That in this contree al the peple sleeth**   **(lines 389–90)**

But the next reference is more sinister, when the innkeeper confirms that:

> **...he hath slain this yeer,**
> **Henne over a mile, withinne a greet village,**
> **Bothe man and womman, child, and hine, and page**
>   **(lines 400–02)**

The reference to the Black Death is unmistakable, with the indiscriminate and inexorable slaughter of whole populations. There is an unpleasant frisson in the assertion that:

> **I trowe his habitacioun be there.**   **(line 403)**

Here Death takes on a more substantial presence, which renders the audience more uneasy at the same time as it makes the rioter's defiance more absurd:

> **Is it swich peril with him for to meete?**   **(line 407)**

To an audience with immediate memories of the Black Death, such bravado would seem grotesque.

Context

Visual images of Death abound in the Middle Ages as constant reminders of man's mortality and the need to repent and to save one's soul. A search on the internet will reveal numerous examples, particularly of the so-called Dance of Death, where skeletons are depicted dancing.

The unnerving quality of the depiction of Death reaches its height with the old man's claim to know Death and to have left him in a grove, as mentioned above. 'Left' can mean 'parted from', but it can also mean that the old man has deliberately placed Death in the grove (in the form of the coins), and the personification finally receives a concrete form. Terror might be too strong a word for a modern audience, but the sense of fear and unease that would be engendered in a medieval audience accustomed to the permanent proximity of death is easy to recognise.

The attractiveness of evil as personified in the Pardoner

Despite, or perhaps because of, his personal grotesqueness, his complete hypocrisy and his unprincipled misuse of his position, the Pardoner remains a fascinating character, and this is a typically Gothic theme. He offers a vicarious insight into a twisted and tortured soul, preaching every day against sin and warning of its eternal consequences, while indulging in precisely the sins he is talking about.

Literature is full of evil figures who seem more interesting than good characters. Satan as portrayed by Milton, Iago in *Othello*, Alex in *A Clockwork Orange* — throughout history authors (and audiences) have been fascinated by the motivations of apparently entirely wicked characters, and it is worth comparing the Pardoner with others in order to consider common features. Daring against odds, panache and style, eloquence and often humour are all elements that can turn the grotesque into the absorbing. True Gothic texts like *Frankenstein* and *Dracula* offer good points of comparison.

The Pardoner's uncertain sexuality equally has a Gothic resonance. Chaucer the pilgrim believes him to be 'a gelding or a mare' ('The General Prologue', line 693), while he apparently sings love duets with the Summoner ('The General Prologue', lines 674–75). This suggestion of homosexuality or emasculation offers ample scope for a modern reader to develop all kinds of theories about the Pardoner's psychological state, which would help to explain his otherwise extraordinary self-exposure. In medieval terms, his latent homosexuality would be a perversion, suggesting the unredeemed corruption of the body. He is outside society, almost outside nature, and so he has little to lose by preying on ordinary men and women.

Task 15

If you are studying the text comparatively, choose a Gothic text and compare the characteristics of the main protagonist with those of the Pardoner.

Context

It can be risky to apply modern psychology to literary texts, especially when the text was written in the distant past, because such readings can severely distort one's interpretation. Nevertheless, it is interesting to look at the possibility of a psychological reading, because, used carefully, it may offer insights.

Characters

The Pardoner in 'The General Prologue'

Even if you are only studying 'The Pardoner's Prologue and Tale', it is essential to examine the description of the Pardoner in 'The General Prologue' as well. This is because he is one of the most completely realised characters in *The Canterbury Tales*, and Chaucer moulds his prologue and tale carefully to suit the character he has set up.

Chaucer moulds his prologue and tale carefully

This is how the Pardoner is introduced in 'The General Prologue' (lines 671–716). The modernised English version (in italics) is entirely literal, and is given to help clarify the meaning of the passage.

With him* ther rood a gentil Pardoner   *the Summoner
With him there rode a worthy Pardoner
Of Rouncivale, his freend and his compeer*,   *close friend
From Rouncivale, his friend and ally,
That streight was comen fro the court of Rome.
Who had come straight from the papal court in Rome.
Ful loude he soong 'Com hider, love, to me!'
Loudly he sang: 'Come hither, love, to me!'
This Somonour bar to him a stif burdoun*;   *bass
The Summoner accompanied him;
Was nevere trompe* of half so greet a soun.   *trumpet
No trumpet was ever half as loud.
This Pardoner hadde heer as yelow as wex,
This Pardoner had hair as yellow as wax,
But smothe it heeng as dooth a strike of flex*;   *flax
But it hung down smoothly like flax;
By ounces* henge his lokkes that he hadde,   *small bunches
What he had hung in loose bunches,
And therwith he his shuldres overspradde;
And he spread these over his shoulders;
But thinne it lay, by colpons* oon and oon.   *strips
But it lay thinly in separate clusters.
But hood, for jolitee, wered he noon,
To appear jolly he didn't wear a hood,
For it was trussed up in his walet*.   *bag
Which was trussed up in his bag.

Hym thoughte he rood al of the newe jet*; *fashion
He thought he rode in the latest fashion;
Dischevelee*, save his cappe*, he rood al bare. *dishevelled *skull-cap
He rode dishevelled and bare-headed apart from his
skull-cap.
Swiche glaringe eyen* hadde he as an hare. *eyes
He had bulging eyes like a hare.
A vernicle* hadde he sowed upon his cappe. *an image of
Saint Veronica
He had a Veronica sewn on his cap.
His walet lay biforn him in his lappe,
His bag lay before him in his lap,
Bretful* of pardoun, comen from Rome al hoot. *brimful
Brimful of pardons hot from Rome.
A voys he hadde as smal* as hath a goot. *high
He had a high voice like a goat.
No berd hadde he, ne nevere sholde have;
He had no beard, and never would have —
As smothe it was as it were late shave.
His skin was smooth as if newly shaved.
I trowe he were a gelding* or a mare. *castrated horse
I think he was a eunuch or a mare.
But of his craft, fro Berwik into Ware,
But as to his craft, from Berwick to Ware
Ne was ther swich another pardoner.
There wasn't a pardoner to match him.
For in his male* he hadde a pilwe-beer*, *bag *pillow-case
In his bag he had a pillow-case
Which that he seyde was Oure Lady veil:
Which he said was Our Lady's veil;
He seyde he hadde a gobet of the seil
He said he had a piece of the sail
That Seint Peter hadde, whan that he wente
That Saint Peter used, when he went
Upon the see, til Jhesu Crist hym hente*. *took
To sea, before Jesus called him.
He hadde a crois of latoun* ful of stones, *brass
He had a brass cross set with stones,
And in a glas* he hadde pigges bones. *case
And in a case he had pigs' bones.
But with thise relikes, whan that he fond
But with these relics, when he found
A povre person* dwellinge upon lond, *priest
A poor priest living in some place,

Upon a day he gat him moore moneye
In one day he made more money
Than that the person gat in monthes tweye;
Than the priest earned in two months.
And thus, with feyned flaterye and japes*,   *tricks
And so, with false flattery and tricks,
He made the person and the peple his apes.
He made monkeys of the priest and people.
But trewely to tellen atte laste,
But to tell truly at the end,
He was in chirche a noble ecclesiaste*.   *cleric
In church he was a noble cleric.
Wel koude he rede a lessoun or a storie,
He knew well how to read a lesson or sermon,
But alderbest* he song an offertorie*;   *best of all *offertory hymn
But best of all he sung the Offertory,
For wel he wiste, whan that song was songe,
For he knew very well that when that song was sung
He moste preche and wel affile* his tonge   *smooth
He must preach and smooth his tongue
To winne silver, as he ful wel koude;
To win silver, as he knew full well how to do.
Therefore he song the murierly* and loude.   *more merrily
Therefore he sung more merrily and louder.

In this portrait, the last of the pilgrims to be described, Chaucer is absolutely uncompromising, in a way rarely found elsewhere in *The Canterbury Tales*. The Pardoner is a loathsome creature, physically repulsive and morally repugnant. His alliance with the Summoner is dubious — he rides with the Summoner, with whom he sings love songs. Chaucer's description of the Summoner has been equally damning, and the image is of a pair of scoundrels. Worse, the Pardoner's lack of manhood suggests that he is the passive partner in an abhorrent homosexual relationship with the Summoner.

The Pardoner's appearance is made revolting. He has lank yellow hair that is thinning, and which hangs down in rats'-tails over his shoulders. He tries to be fashionable, riding bare-headed apart from his religious cap, which has a religious relic pinned to it. He carries other relics and pardons with him. He has glaring eyes like a hare, and he has a tiny high voice and bleats like a goat. He also has no beard and is unlikely to ever have one, because (in the narrator's opinion) he is probably a castrato or even a woman. Despite this he sings and preaches well in church.

The Pardoner is…physically repulsive and morally repugnant

Although Chaucer says there is no other pardoner like him in the whole of England (itself a double-edged remark), his pre-eminence rests in his ability to dupe gullible people through his eloquence and with his false relics. He is a professional pardoner, and the Veronica on his cap advertises his trade. As well as his pardons (indulgences) he has a whole series of false relics, which he uses to trick people out of their money. He travels around, and when he arrives at a place he makes more money in one day than the parish priest can make in two months.

Chaucer does not prevaricate here; he exposes the Pardoner's corrupt practices right away and says that everything he offers is false. Chaucer makes it abundantly clear that the Pardoner is spiritually bankrupt, a defect mirrored by his apparent physical castration. Medieval people believed that a person's physical appearance was a reflection of their inner state. The Pardoner's disgusting appearance indicates his spiritual corruption. He has no redeeming virtues, because although he sings and preaches well, these gifts are used only for personal gain.

*Task **16***

Discuss how well the portrait of the Pardoner in 'The General Prologue' matches what you know of him from 'The Pardoner's Prologue and Tale'. How neatly do the teller and the tale fit together?

The Pardoner in his prologue and tale

'A ful vicious man'

At the end of his prologue the Pardoner states a paradox about his tale:

> **For though myself be a ful vicious man,**
> **A moral tale yet I yow telle kan**   (lines 173–74)

❰ Top ten *quotation*

This is straightforward enough. A story can be independent of its narrator, and its moral worth is not connected to the virtue of its teller. However, there is much more to 'The Pardoner's Prologue and Tale' than this. In his prologue the Pardoner has shown how he uses such tales to gain money — he has already shown that he is corrupt before he narrates his tale. Yet once it is finished, he encourages the pilgrims to buy his wares as if the confession in his prologue had never taken place.

It is worth remembering that 'vicious' should not be taken in its simple modern sense. Here it means, precisely, 'subject to or full of vice' — particularly those vices among the seven deadly sins of which the Pardoner is most guilty: pride, avarice, gluttony, anger and lechery.

The Pardoner's confession

There are alternative responses. One can sympathise with the self-awareness of a man who knows that he is wicked, and who yet achieves good ends in spite of his character. This seems to be the case in lines

143–45, because the Pardoner specifically says that he is able to make people turn away from avarice, despite recognising the sin in himself.

However, the Pardoner who advances this line of reasoning also rejects it. In lines 117–18 he states:

Top ten *quotation* ❯

> **For myn entente is nat but for to winne,**
> **And nothing for correccioun of sinne.**

That is to say, he realises that his sermons may have the effect of turning people from sin, but this is not his intention. He does not care about their souls any more than his own, and is happy for them to be damned:

Top ten *quotation* ❯

> **I rekke nevere, whan that they been beried,**
> **Though that hir soules goon a-blakeberied.**   (lines 119–20)

Task 17

Discuss with other students how far the Pardoner can be seen as attractive or admirable, and how far he is loathsome. Be prepared to defend your point of view through reference to the text.

Here is a portrait of true corruption. The Pardoner is not excused by the fact that he was part of a corrupt system. Although he works solely for his own profit, the Church must have been fully aware of the dishonest methods of licensed pardoners, and condoned such practices where it enriched the Church. Chaucer's satirical portrait of a corrupt institution is focused through this single character.

The attempt to dupe the pilgrims

At the very end of his tale, with the story of the rioters concluded but fresh in mind, the Pardoner makes a sudden attempt to get the pilgrims to buy his services. Again, it is worth exploring alternative interpretations of this passage. One reading is that the Pardoner is so conceited that he reckons he can pull off the ultimate confidence trick, by revealing his trade secrets and then still brazenly demanding that the pilgrims take the bait. Such a view would mean that the Pardoner holds the pilgrims in complete contempt. When he provokingly suggests that the Host should begin because 'he is moost envoluped in sinne' (line 656), he picks on the least intellectually astute of the pilgrims. He perhaps hopes that the other pilgrims will laugh at the Host — but if the Host comes forward and buys a pardon, others are likely to follow suit. In this reading, the Host's rebuke comes as a horrid shock to the Pardoner, suggesting that the Host is not as stupid as he seems, or that the Pardoner is not as capable as he believes.

Context

You should not view the Pardoner's corruption in isolation. The medieval Church was corrupt in many ways; simony (selling ecclesiastical positions) and nepotism (offering positions to one's relatives) were rife, and medieval popes were frequently among the most corrupt of all. A little research will demonstrate this very easily.

An alternative explanation is that the Pardoner truly believes he can deceive the pilgrims; that he is so monstrously obsessed by his own skills that he thinks the pilgrims will fail to spot the significance of his confession. The Pardoner is driven by pride, the chief of the seven deadly sins, and this sin leads to a false sense of personal worth and capabilities (the rioters are similarly guilty). This reading may also take into account the fact that the Pardoner has insisted on drinking before he starts his tale (lines 41–42 and 170–72), and so overestimates his powers and maybe fails to notice how much he has given away. The rude awakening is much the same in this case, for the Host's retort proves that the Pardoner is deluded in a way that the Pardoner cannot mistake.

The Pardoner's own soul

This is a curious aspect of the tale. A more modern Pardoner might adopt an agnostic or atheistic position about the nature of the soul, of heaven and hell. He might consciously or unconsciously reject the notion of eternal damnation, and thus justify his own procedures to himself. This could hardly have been true, however, in the Middle Ages. True atheism, and even agnosticism, were not available philosophical positions. God existed, heaven and hell existed; the fate of one's immortal soul depended on what a person did in his or her lifetime.

What Chaucer presents is a godless man — a man so far turned from God that he no longer cares about the eternal consequences of his actions. He is a true criminal — a man who understands the evil of what he is doing, who knows the consequences, and yet who continues with his crimes anyway. This is not an uncommon phenomenon in everyday life, but it is exemplary to see how Chaucer presents a character who follows this course to its logical end. He functions as a pardoner, dealing in salvation and the amelioration of sin, yet he will not turn away from sin himself.

The Pardoner can be compared to Satan, who as Lucifer was an angel in heaven, but who chose to defy God and was cast down into hell. The Pardoner has a position of trust, and could work for the good of others, but he prefers to defy God and serve only himself. His reward, like Satan's, will be eternal damnation.

The Pardoner's psychology

A modern reader is at liberty to construct psychological theories about the Pardoner. He can be seen as deluded or deranged; he may be considered to have an inadequate or damaged personality that seeks self-expression through the most provocative and outrageous behaviour. He always has to compete, and he always has to win — which is why his failure at the very end is so devastating for him. His uncertain sexuality, with a possible homoerotic relationship with the Summoner, offers further ground for consideration and discussion from a modern psychoanalytic perspective. All such theories can accommodate and make sense of his final challenge to the pilgrims, and his chagrin at

*Task **18***

Create a presentation for your class or group outlining the alternative interpretations of the Pardoner's behaviour, together with your own view of the matter.

being repulsed is certainly very naturalistic: 'So wrooth he was, no word ne wolde he seye' (line 671).

The Pardoner's sexuality

Chaucer calls into the question the Pardoner's sexuality right back in 'The General Prologue': 'I trowe he were a gelding or a mare' (line 693).

This uncompromising statement is clearly meant to have symbolic significance, but the full force of it is not necessarily straightforward for a modern reader to recover.

In a simple sense, Chaucer may be providing a metaphor for the Pardoner's spiritual sterility. He is spiritually barren, dead to the Word of God and the awful implications of what he is doing. He confesses to mortal sin, but takes no steps to redeem himself. He subverts his sacred function by selling false pardons and offering false relics. He is even happy for others to go to hell, provided he makes his profit.

A second significance of his sterility might be in relation to medieval notions of manhood. He is part of a patriarchal society, where men rule and women are subservient. The suggestion of his effeminacy ('a mare') would put him beneath all other men, unfit to play his proper role in society. The possibility of a homosexual relationship with the Summoner, with whom he sings love songs, would have been even more abhorrent. Homosexuality was seen as a vile sin by the Catholic Church, an attitude persisting to our own times in some quarters.

This lack of manhood might, where a psychological reading of the Pardoner is taken, partly account for his behaviour. The pilgrimage is full of strong, apparently successful men — the Knight, the Monk, the Host. Inadequate himself, the Pardoner gains his revenge on society and the hierarchy of his times by abusing his position and laughing at all those whom he fools: 'He made the person and the peple his apes' ('The General Prologue', line 708).

His choice of the Host as a target at the end of his tale is consonant with this view. If he can get the better of a virile and dominant man, he can prove his own worth. As it is, he is horribly rebuffed.

The Pardoner as a literary construct

Equally, the Pardoner may be understood as a purely literary construct, with no 'personality' or psychology in a modern sense. This would state that Chaucer has constructed the figure purely in order to exemplify a characteristic, for example the sin of pride, and that the Pardoner has

Taking it Further ▶

The most famous example of a psychoanalytic reading of a literary text is Ernest Jones' work on *Hamlet*. It is worth reading this to see whether it has merit as a way of approaching 'The Pardoner's Prologue and Tale'. Extracts from the article can be found at http://shakespeare-navigators.com//jones/

no more reality than the allegorical characters in the medieval morality plays or in Bunyan's *The Pilgrim's Progress*. In this case, every aspect of his prologue and tale are exemplifications of a character type, and the ending of his tale is not meant to seem naturalistic or probable — that is not its function. Its purpose is to show how deeply self-deluding a sinful soul can be.

There is no conflict between this interpretation and the portrayal of the Pardoner in realistic terms. Items like the husband's sudden blindness in 'The Merchant's Tale' or the behaviour of 'patient Griselda' in 'The Clerk's Tale' are adequate proof that Chaucer was able to combine a high degree of realism with entirely symbolic events.

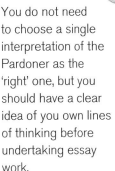

*Pause for **Thought***

You do not need to choose a single interpretation of the Pardoner as the 'right' one, but you should have a clear idea of you own lines of thinking before undertaking essay work.

The rioters and the old man

Part of the power of 'The Pardoner's Tale' is that it is simultaneously naturalistic and evidently symbolic. Chaucer's writing gives it a naturalistic feel; the quest for Death indicates that we are to look for symbolic meaning throughout. This is evident when we look at the main characters — the three rioters, and the old man they meet. In each case there is a range of interpretations that are worth exploring.

The rioters: possible interpretations

Individuals

Chaucer takes great care to make the rioters seem like ordinary people. Their speech is colloquial:

> **Ey! Goddes precious dignitee! who wende**
> **To-day that we sholde han so fair a grace?**   (lines 496–97)

and they behave like ordinary friends:

> **Herkneth, felawes, we thre been al ones;**
> **Lat ech of us holde up his hand til oother**
> **And ech of us bicomen otheres brother**   (lines 410–12)

Their drunken boast that they will kill Death is all too human:

> **He shal be slain, he that so manye sleeth,**
> **By Goddes dignitee, er it be night.**   (lines 414–15)

A trinity

The fact that there are three rioters adds an ominous layer of symbolism to the tale. To a Christian mind, the number three is inescapably linked

Taking it
Further

The number three has significance in most major religious and cultural contexts. Explore its significance in a Christian and western European context.

with the Holy Trinity — God the Father, God the Son and God the Holy Ghost. The rioters instantly form a kind of anti-trinity. They mock the true Trinity through their blasphemy; they mock it through their treachery and betrayal of one another. In a simpler sense, a trio of friends or siblings is a traditional feature of folk tales and fairy stories, and allows conflict where two gang up against the third (who in this case ironically defeats them).

Sinners

In the context of the Pardoner's digression on sin, lines 197–374, it is clear that we are to take the rioters as being representative of sinful men:

> They daunce and pleyen at dees bothe day and night,
> And eten also and drinken over hir might   (lines 181–82)

> Hir othes been so grete and so dampnable
> That it is grisly for to heere hem swere.   (lines 186–87)

They are also so steeped in sin that the devil may easily tempt them to murder:

> And atte laste the feend, oure enemy,
> Putte in his thought that he sholde poison beye
>
>   (lines 558–59)

The Pardoner's final rhetorical flourish confirms that the rioters are archetypally sinners:

> O cursed sinne of alle cursednesse!
> O traitours homicide, O wikkednesse!   (lines 609–10)

All of us

To the medieval mind, all men are sinners, because all share in the Original Sin of Adam and Eve, from which Christ redeemed mankind. It is simple to see, therefore, that the Pardoner's audience was expected to perceive in his sermon faults that the listeners might easily be guilty of themselves. That is why he can move directly from his tale of the revellers to the sins of his auditors:

> Now, goode men, God foryeve yow youre trespas,
> And ware yow fro the sinne of avarice!   (lines 618–19)

The first line has its direct reference to the Lord's Prayer, 'forgive us our trespasses', in which all Christians admit their sinful nature, before the Pardoner focuses specifically on the deadly sin of avarice (it should be noted that the reference to 'goode men' in line 618 is mere politeness, like 'gentlemen', and does not imply that the audience is morally good).

It may take a little effort for a modern audience, not necessarily Christian and not necessarily brought up with a notion of universal sinfulness, to reconstruct the mindset of the original audiences for the Pardoner's sermon, both fictitious and real. It is necessary, however, to realise the significance of the point, because it is on this basis that the Pardoner can justify offering his pardons and relics to a believing audience.

Task **19**

In class or in an essay, discuss the alternative readings of the rioters' roles.

The old man: possible interpretations

An individual

As with the rioters, Chaucer paints a vivid picture. The old man responds to the oafishness of the rioters politely and with dignity:

> But sires, to yow it is no curteisye
> To speken to an old man vileynye   (lines 453–54)

At the same time the irony of his response is clear when they abusively ask him why he is still alive:

> …For I ne kan nat finde/A man,…
> That wolde chaunge his youthe for myn age.
>   (lines 435–36, 438)

Old age/mortality

He is described as 'an olde man' (line 427) as soon as the rioters meet him, but the symbolic representation is confirmed later:

> Lo how I vanisshe, flessh and blood and skin!
> Allas! whan shul my bones been at reste?   (lines 446–47)

Even more striking is the image of him knocking on the ground, seeking to die:

> And on the ground, which is my moodres gate,
> I knokke with my staf, bothe erly and late,
> And seye, "Leeve mooder, leet me in!"   (lines 443–45)

◀ Top ten *quotation*

The voice of wisdom

There is an important and simple distinction between the 'old man' and the 'yonge folk that haunteden folye' (line 178). It was conventional that old age brought wisdom, and that young people should listen to their elders. It is perhaps equally conventional that the young people pay no attention. The old man speaks politely to them and tells them only the truth, but they abuse him and ignore what he says. It is only when they persist in their folly that he points the way to Death.

The Wandering Jew

There was a popular medieval legend about the Wandering Jew. The exact origins of the legend are debatable, but concern a figure, perhaps a man who insulted Jesus on the way to his Crucifixion, who was cursed and doomed to remain alive and wander the Earth to await the second coming of Christ.

There is no direct suggestion in 'The Pardoner's Tale' that the old man represents the Wandering Jew, but Chaucer may have taken from a current popular legend the powerful image of a cursed man who wants to die but cannot do so.

Death's accomplice

This is the easiest association to find:

Top ten *quotation*

> 'Now, sires,' quod he, 'if that yow be so leef
> To finde Deeth, turne up this croked wey,
> For in that grove I lafte him, by my fey   (lines 474–76)

He directs the rioters to their death, knowing full well what will happen if they turn onto the 'croked wey'. However, it should be noted that he only says this after they have provoked and abused him. In line 463 he intends to leave without giving them directions.

Task 20

In class or in an essay, discuss the alternative readings of the old man's role.

Death

This is just an extension of the previous interpretation, and rests on the same evidence. Death was conventionally represented in art as a male hooded skeleton figure, so a skeletal-looking old man would be a near image. If the old man represents mortality anyway, it is easy to visualise the macabre image of a death figure pointing the way to death itself.

The Devil

Top ten *quotation*

The old man manifestly tempts the rioters into mortal sin. He points the way to them, and states that it is a 'croked wey', the path of sin. The image is strongly biblical — Paul in the Acts of the Apostles (Chapter 13, verse 10) accuses the sorcerer Elymas of making crooked the straight ways of the Lord. The Pardoner's (and Chaucer's) audiences would have been in no doubt about the symbolic force of the image. The old man sits beside a stile (line 426), which symbolically represents a decision point. The rioters turn aside from the true way and rush to their deaths.

Gullible characters

The Pardoner's success depends on his ability to make people believe what he says, that is to say on their degree of credulity. This idea becomes one of Chaucer's central concerns in 'The Pardoner's Prologue and Tale'. Being Chaucer, he examines the issue from several angles.

The rioters in 'The Pardoner's Tale'

The rioters are easily deceived. Despite being warned by the serving-boy about the danger of meeting Death, the rioters are contemptuous: 'Is it swich peril with him for to meete?' (line 407).

This classic example of a rhetorical question shows the depth of the rioters' ignorance and arrogance. When the old man directs them up the 'croked wey', they rush off to meet their death without a thought, unaware of the distinction between the appearance of the situation and its reality.

❮ Top ten **quotation**

The Pardoner's usual audience

A similar failure characterises the usual audience for one of the Pardoner's sermons, but at least they have an excuse. They fear for their immortal souls, and knowing themselves sinners, it is natural that they should seek redemption for their actions and even insurance for what they might do. Blessed relics, they believe, have holy powers and can cure ills and protect them:

> **Taak water of that welle and wassh his tonge,**
> **And it is hool anon...**   **(lines 70–71)**

Indulgences could alleviate the punishment for their sins, or even excuse them from punishment altogether: 'Myn hooly pardoun may yow alle warice' (line 620).

When the soul is at stake, it is understandable that people would clutch at the opportunities the Pardoner offers them. Their failure to consider whether the Pardoner's claims are genuine is forgivable.

*Pause for **Thought***

What anxieties do you possess yourself for which you seek some kind of spiritual reassurance or comfort?

The Pardoner himself

Thus far, people's gullibility is straightforward, motivated by pride (in the case of the rioters) or fear (in the case of the Pardoner's normal audience). Chaucer extends the theme, however, by making the Pardoner himself fallible. For some reason — arguably through pride — the Pardoner believes he can dupe the pilgrims to whom he has just made his confession. He too fails to distinguish the true situation. He believes

that the Host is gullible enough to fall for his tricks, even after he has exposed the mechanism. He is dumbfounded by the Host's retort:

> **This Pardoner answerde nat a word;**
> **So wrooth he was, no word ne wolde he seye. (lines 670–71)**

The Canterbury pilgrims

It is Chaucer's irony that makes the pilgrims the clear-sighted figures in 'The Pardoner's Tale'. If the Host, among the most literal and least perceptive of the pilgrims, can see through the Pardoner's attempt to con him so easily, then we are meant to understand that the pilgrims are sophisticated enough to distinguish truth from lies, unlike the Pardoner's usual audiences. This is not lessened by the Pardoner's earlier confession — he still attempts to dupe them at the end. The reaction of the pilgrims is the worst reaction the Pardoner can receive — 'al the peple lough' (line 675) at him. This is the nature of Chaucer's satire — exposing folly and vice through laughter at it.

Chaucer's audience

By extension, Chaucer's audience vicariously shares in the Host's scathing denunciation of the Pardoner. This makes the audience members feel superior, in that they have not been deceived by the Pardoner's tricks either, and they can laugh at the gullibility of others. They appreciate in full Chaucer's satirical intent, and the way that the Pardoner's hollowness has been exposed.

The Host and the Pardoner

The Host has a crucial role in any analysis of the Pardoner, because his comments form a frame within which 'The Pardoner's Prologue and Tale' take place and are judged. Prior to the Pardoner's prologue comes its introduction, forming a bridge between the previous (Physician's) tale and the Pardoner's contribution. The introduction consists of the Host's response to 'The Physician's Tale', followed by him calling on the Pardoner to tell the pilgrims some 'mirthe or japes' (line 33). At the end of 'The Pardoner's Tale', the Pardoner famously calls on the Host to come forward first because he is 'moost envoluped in sinne' (line 656). The Host's reply forms the conclusion of 'The Pardoner's Prologue and Tale'.

The Pardoner is preceded in *The Canterbury Tales* by a doctor, who tells 'The Physician's Tale'. This is a very short story (286 lines) about a beautiful maiden named Virginia who accepts death (at her father's hand) rather than having to lose her virginity to an evil man. The Host, whose name is Harry Bailly, responds to 'The Physician's Tale' with ready humanity and sympathy. He feels as much for the fictional characters depicted in it as he does for real people. He lacks critical perceptiveness and acuity — he tends to take things at face value. He feels strong sympathy for the innocent girl: 'Allas, so pitously as she was slain!' (line 12), and similarly strong condemnation of the guilty individuals: 'This was a fals cherl and a fals justise' (line 3). He freely admits this emotional response: 'But wel I woot thou doost myn herte to erme' (line 26), and that unless there is a remedy 'Myn herte is lost for pitee of this maide' (line 31). It may be this simplicity that causes the Pardoner to choose the Host as a target at the end of his tale.

The Pardoner seriously misjudges the Host at the end of his tale. He seems to think that, because the Host takes things literally and does not see the more sophisticated moral significance of what he hears, he will overlook the Pardoner's confession of his own corruption. The outcome is wildly comic. The Host is not nearly as limited as the Pardoner thinks, and responds violently to the suggestion that he is the most sinful of the pilgrims. His anger is manifested in a graphic insult:

> **I wolde I hadde thy coillons in myn hond**
> **In stide of relikes or of seintuarie.**
> **Lat kutte hem of, I wol thee helpe hem carie;**
> **They shul be shrined in an hogges toord!**   **(lines 666–69)**

The scathing brutality of this renders the Pardoner speechless, itself a surprise event. The Host has recognised the falsehood of the Pardoner's relics and his claims. Additionally, he seems to have picked up on the pilgrim Chaucer's suggestion that the Pardoner may be a eunuch — the suggestion of cutting off his testicles is doubly abusive when it appears that the Pardoner may not have any. The parody of religious ceremony, with the suggestion of treating the testicles as relics themselves, 'shrined in an hogges toord', is brazen and comical.

It is salutary to note that the rhetorical and verbal sophistication of the Pardoner has been completely undone by the Host's coarse vocabulary — 'coillons', 'toord'. His earthy rejoinder invites the audience to consider its own response to the Pardoner and what he has to say.

Task 21

Write the text of an interview with the Host, either at the end of the Introduction, or at the end of the Tale, or both. Aim to capture a sense of the Host's individual voice, and his opinion of the Pardoner.

❮ Top ten *quotation*

❮ Top ten *quotation*

Form, structure and language

This section is designed to offer you information about the three strands of AO2. This Assessment Objective requires you to demonstrate detailed critical understanding in analysing the ways in which form, structure and language shape meanings in literary texts. To a certain extent, these three terms should, as indicated elsewhere, be seen as fluid and interactive. Remember, however, that in the analysis of a work such as *The Canterbury Tales*, aspects of form and structure are at least as important as language. You should not focus your study merely on lexical features of the text. Many features of form, structure and language in 'The Pardoner's Prologue and Tale' are further explored in this guide in the *Summaries and commentaries* and in exemplar essays.

Form

'The Pardoner's Tale' is a poetic narrative written in rhyming couplets of iambic pentameter, narrated by the Pardoner, one of the pilgrim characters in *The Canterbury Tales*. It is preceded by a prologue, in the same poetic form, where the Pardoner talks about his methods of preaching.

You are in an unusual position when studying 'The Pardoner's Prologue and Tale' for examination purposes, because the text is set in isolation. It forms a tiny part of a much larger whole, *The Canterbury Tales*, and you cannot hope to understand 'The Pardoner's Prologue and Tale' without a clear sense of this immediate context. 'The Pardoner's Tale' is one story in a large collection of stories (Chaucer originally intended there to be 120 of them, of which he wrote 24). There is plenty of material in this guide to help you, but you should aim to look at a copy of the complete *Canterbury Tales* in order to get a sense of its size and purpose. You will immediately discover that 'The Pardoner's Prologue and Tale' is itself unusual within the context of *The Canterbury Tales*: whereas most of the tales in the collection have no introduction or a very short one, in the case of the Pardoner his prologue is extended to 100 lines, by the end of which we have a considerable insight into his character and personality,

Taking it Further ▶

Study one of the modernised versions of *The Canterbury Tales* in order to see the variety of tales in the collection and how 'The Pardoner's Prologue and Tale' fits into it.

to add to what we already know from 'The General Prologue'. The only comparable character is the Wife of Bath, another memorable and loquacious figure, who takes 800 lines to introduce herself.

It should be noted that the Pardoner's story of the three rioters is not original — very few of *The Canterbury Tales* are. The basic story of the young men who quarrel and end up killing one another is as old as literature itself, and seems to have originated as one of the Jataka tales in India. What Chaucer does — and in this sense he shares much in common with Shakespeare — is to take a well-known story and adapt it to fit his particular context and purposes. In the same way that Shakespeare deepens the source text for *Hamlet* to create a profound study of the melancholy prince, so Chaucer takes a folk tale, darkens it with the powerful and ambiguous figure of the old man, and manipulates it so that it becomes a commentary on the nature of its teller.

Multiple narrators

You should read this in conjunction with the *Contexts* section, 'The multiple narrator in the *Tales*' on pp. 74–76 of this guide.

'The Pardoner's Prologue and Tale' features a common device in the shape of the 'unreliable narrator'; that is to say, a narrator whose personal and partial viewpoint means that the audience cannot accept anything he says on trust, unlike a conventional novel where the 'omniscient narrator' truthfully directs what the reader needs to know. Your response to 'The Pardoner's Prologue and Tale' must be a complex one, because of the layers of narrative that take place. The Pardoner is one of Chaucer's most vivid creations, so this makes the issue of multiple narration a key one when studying his prologue and tale. In every line you need to look behind the character of the Pardoner to consider what effect Chaucer the author is trying to achieve. In the case of 'The Pardoner's Prologue and Tale' you need not concern yourself with the persona of Chaucer as a pilgrim narrator — he is not 'visible'. The issue is to decide whether Chaucer is presenting the Pardoner as a man, evil perhaps but fallibly human, or as an embodiment of unpalatable views and attitudes.

In many ways this is the single most important question in defining your response to 'The Pardoner's Prologue and Tale', but is dependent on a view of *The Canterbury Tales* beyond the immediate confines of the Pardoner's section. This is where studying the Pardoner in isolation is limiting and judgements need to be made with caution. Your response is an entirely personal matter, but it will depend on the preconceptions

Taking it Further

The sources of 'The Pardoner's Tale' can be explored in an article by W. A. Clouston. To find this, type 'Chaucer originals and analogues' into Google; then select the reference 'Originals and Analogues of Some of Chaucer's Canterbury Tales' by Frederick James Furnivall. The article is on pp. 415–36, and includes a summary of the original tale from the Vedabha Jataka.

you bring to the study of Chaucer, the breadth of your knowledge of *The Canterbury Tales* and its background to put the Pardoner's contribution in context, and your depth of understanding of 'The Pardoner's Prologue and Tale' itself. The one safe thing that may be said is that no simplistic answer will do. It is not true that the Pardoner is an embodiment of medieval vice, any more than that he is a fully realised individual character. It is through extended study, discussion and thought that you will be able to develop the informed judgement required for A-level. A single example will suffice to show the kind of consideration that needs to be given to the text throughout:

> Now, goode men, God foryeve yow youre trespas,
> And ware you fro the sinne of avarice!   (lines 618–19)

A sophisticated response is required here. Taken out of context the lines seem an entirely conventional admonition, including as they do an almost direct quotation from the Lord's Prayer ('forgive us our trespasses'). As words from a preacher, they have this admonitory force, and seem a natural conclusion to the Pardoner's story. However, it is evident that not all is as it seems. We are aware that the Pardoner has confessed to precisely the sin of avarice against which he is now warning us. Is he sincere, or hypocritical? Sincerity would suggest to some readers the complexities of the Pardoner's psyche and soul, a man struggling with his own nature, aware of his own damnation but capable of warning others against it. If on the other hand he is hypocritical, laughing at the audience whom he intends to fleece, then the lines are a powerful satirical indictment of the depth of the Pardoner's depravity.

The audience needs to consider these alternative interpretations. Also, if the lines are hypocritical, then the audience needs to hold on to that aspect, while simultaneously being aware that Chaucer would mean an audience to accept their straightforward moral force. Modern students sometimes assume that medieval literature will be simple because it is old. Nothing could be further from the truth.

Task **22**

Summarise, perhaps in graphic or tabular form, the arguments for and against various views of the Pardoner, and compare these with those of other students.

Structure

For the modern student studying 'The Pardoner's Prologue and Tale', the text has something of the quality of a set of Russian dolls. At the centre is the moral tale of the three rioters which the Pardoner tells. This is contained in the wider context of the whole of the Pardoner's speech, including his prologue and his own introduction to the tale. This in turn is framed by the Host's introduction and concluding comments. Finally, all this is part of the much larger context of *The Canterbury Tales* as a whole, of which 'The Pardoner's Prologue and Tale' forms a tiny section. You need to bear these contexts permanently in mind as you study.

The specific structure of 'The Pardoner's Prologue and Tale' is discussed at length in the *Summaries and Commentaries* section of this guide, pp. 6–22, and so is only briefly summarised here. You need to think of the prologue and tale as forming a single organic whole with a bipartite structure. 'The Pardoner's Prologue' is in the form of a confession, a personal account of the Pardoner's behaviour and actions, modelled around the theme of '*Radix malorum est Cupiditas*'. The story that the Pardoner tells is then an *exemplum* designed to illustrate this theme with a practical example. The two are bridged by the Pardoner's comments on a number of sins at the beginning of 'The Pardoner's Tale'. This lengthy passage, lines 197–374 of the tale, not only reinforces the moral message of the rest of the text, but also acts brilliantly as a dramatic device to increase suspense by delaying the telling of the story proper. For nearly 200 lines, after a tantalising opening, the audience is kept waiting for the story to begin. When it does so in line 375 the abruptness of the commencement is noticeable, and the story itself is told with great economy and brevity. This gives it powerful impact, but when viewed dispassionately, it can be seen that Chaucer intends us to view it as only a part of the overall 'Pardoner's Prologue and Tale', which should be considered as a unity. That in turn, properly understood, is only an aspect of the study of virtue and vice that is *The Canterbury Tales*.

❮ Top ten *quotation*

Task 23

Create a diagram in pictorial form to represent the nesting layers of the text, in order to clarify your own understanding of the structure.

Language

Chaucer's verse

The metre that Chaucer adopted for most of *The Canterbury Tales* became the standard one used in English poetry for the next 500 years, and in this sense at least, he should be familiar to the modern reader. He writes in iambic pentameter, the metre used by Shakespeare, Milton, Keats and all the great poets prior to the twentieth century. The lines are arranged into pairs called heroic couplets, a grand style often undermined by its content.

'Iambic' refers to the rhythm of the verse: a repeated pattern of two syllables, with the first syllable being unstressed and the second syllable

being stressed, as in words like 'remind' and 'believe'. An iamb is one of these two-syllable, unstressed/stressed patterns. Each pair of syllables is called a foot. 'Pentameter' (literally five measures or 'feet') means that five feet are joined together to make a ten-syllable (decasyllabic) regular line: da dum da dum da dum da dum da dum. The conventional mark for a stressed syllable is /, and the mark for an unstressed syllable is ~. A couplet of iambic pentameter therefore goes like this:

> ~ / ~ / ~ / ~ / ~ /
> **Bifil that in that seson on a day,**
>
> ~ / ~ / ~ / ~ / ~ /
> **In Southwerk at the Tabard as I lay**
>
> ('The General Prologue', lines 19–20)

iambic rhythm is closest to natural speech

The reason that this became the staple metre of English poetry is because iambic rhythm is closest to natural speech — whenever you speak a sentence, it contains more iambs than any other rhythm. Chaucer shows astonishing assurance and versatility in handling the iambic form. He can use it for formal description in a stately manner:

> **In Flaundres whilom was a compaignye**
> **Of yonge folk that haunteden folye,**
> **As riot, hasard, stywes, and tavernes**
>
> ('The Pardoner's Tale', lines 177–79)

He can use it for fast-paced action:

> **And with that word it happed him, par cas,**
> **To take the botel ther the poison was,**
> **And drank, and yaf his felawe drinke also,**
> **For which anon they storven bothe two.**
>
> (ibid., lines 599–602)

He uses it for rhetorical effect:

> **O cursed sinne of alle cursednesse!**
> **O traitours homicide, O wikkednesse!**
> **O glotonye, luxurie, and hasardrye!**   (ibid., lines 609–11)

But most frequently and most effectively he uses it to represent speech:

> **Lo, how deere, shortly for to sayn,**
> **Aboght was thilke cursed vileynye**   (ibid., lines 216–17)
>
> **'Nay, nay,' quod he, 'thanne have I Cristes curs!**
> **Lat be,' quod he, 'it shal nat be, so theech!**
>
> (ibid., lines 660–61)

In his earlier work, Chaucer frequently used an octosyllabic (eight-syllable) line, which was common at the time; the iambic pentameter marks his maturity as a poet.

Chaucer's language

There is no doubt that the Middle English of *The Canterbury Tales* comes between the modern reader and an easy appreciation of the work. However, after a little practice most of the difficulties presented by the language drop away. Note that the vocabulary can present problems, because some words look familiar or obvious yet are not. For example, the word 'wood' can mean wood but, in a different context, means mad, as in the description of the Host in the 'Introduction to The Pardoner's Tale' (line 1). The solution is to keep a careful eye on the notes and glossary of your edition.

Reading aloud

The easiest way to start to understand Chaucer's language is to read it aloud, or to listen to it being read. Chaucer intended his verse to be spoken, and it makes more sense when it is. Remember the following:

- Most letters are pronounced, so that 'knight' sounds like 'cnicht' and 'mighte' like 'micht'.
- The final 'e' on words like 'fooles' ('fool-es') is normally pronounced, unless it is followed by another vowel.
- Some vowels have different sound values, but do not worry about this initially.
- Words imported from French would still sound French, so 'dotage' would be 'dough-targe' and 'mariage' would be 'mar-ee-arge'.

With these few simple adjustments, aim to read the verse as if it were ordinary conversation. Try to ignore the rhythm and rhyme — they will take care of themselves. Your edition should have further detail on aspects of pronunciation, but the primary objective is to get a sense of the flow of the language.

Modernisations

Another good way of gaining confidence in reading the language is to create a Modern English version of each line. This can be done aloud in class, or you can jot down a literal version as you go along, for example:

In Flaundres whilom was a compaignye

Task 24

Find your own examples of different ways in which Chaucer uses the verse form; be prepared to use such examples in your essays.

> *In Flanders once upon a time there was a group*
> *Of yonge folk that haunteden folye*
> *Of young people who behaved foolishly*

It is not long before Chaucer's English becomes almost as straightforward as Shakespeare's. You never quite lose your caution in looking at it (as you should not with Shakespeare), but you do become more comfortable working with it.

It may be a good idea to obtain a modern version of 'The Pardoner's Prologue and Tale', and even of the whole of *The Canterbury Tales*. This will allow you to check your own rendering of each line, so that you are confident that you have the correct basic meaning.

The Pardoner's use of language

The Pardoner...
knows how
to engage an
audience

The Pardoner is a professional speaker — he is used to preaching, and knows how to engage an audience. Apart from the Parson, he is the most accomplished public speaker amongst the pilgrims.

Chaucer makes him eloquent, but varies his speech from the formal and rhetorical nature of his preaching to the casual conversational style he uses with the other pilgrims. It is this blending of the formal and the informal that gives the character of the Pardoner such complexity and apparent realism. Every line offers potential examples for discussion, so the following are offered only as starting points.

Conversational style

This is most evident at those moments when he is speaking to the other pilgrims, at the end of the introduction and at the end of his prologue.

> 'I graunte, ywis,' quod he, 'but I moot thinke
> Upon som honest thing while that I drinke.'   (lines 41–42)

> But herkneth, lordinges, in conclusioun:
> Youre liking is that I shal telle a tale.   (lines 168–69)

Colloquial words and phrases

It shal be doon.	(line 34)
alle and some	(line 50)
a-blakeberied	(line 120)
Now hoold youre pees!	(line 176)
a stiked swyn	(line 270)

Top ten *quotation* ⟩

PHILIP ALLAN LITERATURE GUIDE **FOR A-LEVEL**

Conversational sentence structures

Allas, a foul thing is it, by my feith,
To seye this word, and fouler is the dede   (lines 238–39)

But herkneth, lordinges, o word, I yow preye.   (line 287)

Rhetoric

The Pardoner, as a professional speaker, makes much use of the rhetorical techniques that were an intrinsic part of medieval education, and which were developed systematically in the Middle Ages by writers such as Geoffrey of Vinsauf. Rhetoric was one of the seven liberal arts taught in universities. It is not necessary for you to be familiar with the classical terms such as *occupatio*, *amplificatio* and *abbreviatio*, but you should be able to recognise features.

Rhetorical questions are instantly visible: 'What nedeth it to sermone of it moore?' (line 593).

The whole of his tale involves *amplificatio*, the gradual accretion of material to add emphasis and force to an idea. Most striking of all is the Pardoner's frequent use of *exclamatio*, or more precisely *ecphonesis*, that is to say emotional exclamation. It features in lines 212–14, line 248 and line 265, but these are all in a way preparatory to the grand finale to his story in lines 609–11.

Exempla

The most noticeably formal and rhetorical aspect of 'The Pardoner's Tale' is the way he uses lists of examples — *exempla* — to support his case. This may seem unusual to modern eyes, but was commonplace in medieval literature, where authorities counted for so much. Having begun his story about the 'compaignye/Of yonge folk' (lines 177–78), the Pardoner interposes a series of *exempla* to develop his theme. This occupies lines 197–374. The Bible is his main source, but he ranges freely across Classical and later authorities, from Seneca to John of Salisbury.

Formal vocabulary

It is obvious that the Pardoner will use technical terms associated with his vocation — 'theme' (line 47), 'patente' (line 51), 'predicacioun' (line 59), 'ensamples' (line 149). He also uses formal vocabulary to make himself sound superior — for example 'hauteyn' (line 44), 'pronounce' (line 49) and 'saffron' (line 59). He also claims he uses Latin (line 58), particularly in stating his theme (line 48).

Taking it ➤ *Further* ➤

Explore the importance of rhetoric in the Middle Ages and look at some of the devices used by Chaucer and other writers. A website such as 'The Forest of Rhetoric' (do an internet search on this, or go to: http://humanities. byu.edu/rhetoric/silva. htm) is invaluable here, and will give an insight into a subject which was one of the seven liberal arts taught in medieval universities, although it receives little or no emphasis in modern education.

Formal sentence structures

His use of formal sentence structures is evident throughout his prologue and tale, never more so than in the storytelling 'once upon a time' opening of his tale:

> In Flaundres whilom was a compaignye
> Of yonge folk that haunteden folye   (lines 177–78)

The Pardoner's voice

It can be disputed whether Chaucer gives the Pardoner an individual voice. The Pardoner is not as immediately distinctive as the Wife of Bath, for example, whose free-flowing and garrulous utterance is brilliantly depicted by Chaucer. Much of his speech is conscious and formal, both in his prologue and his tale. At the same time, the depth and brazenness of his self-confession resonates and remains highly memorable:

Task 25

Identify further examples of places where the Pardoner seems to you to have a distinctive, individual voice. In each case explain how Chaucer has achieved the effect.

Top ten *quotation* 〉

> Thus spitte I out my venym under hewe
> Of hoolinesse, to semen hooly and trewe.   (lines 135–36)

This seems to catch an individual voice — the image of the Pardoner 'spitting' poison like a snake; the repetition of 'holy' in the second line to emphasise the deceit that he uses. The Pardoner may eventually be a literary figure composed in a non-naturalistic age, but he comes across to the modern reader as a fully realised character. The combination of homely image and God-defying arrogance in lines 119–20 are sharply effective in giving the impression of a true individual:

> I rekke nevere, whan that they been beried,
> Though that hir soules goon a-blakeberied.

Humour

Much of *The Canterbury Tales* is meant to be entertaining, even where it contains serious moral points. Chaucer's use of irony is dealt with on pp. 56–59 of this guide, but he uses other techniques as well.

Parody

The Pardoner's story of the three rioters can be seen as a parody of a conventional medieval knightly quest.

- **The questers** Traditionally, quests were undertaken by knights, who were of noble birth, chivalrous, Christian and devout. In the Pardoner's story the rioters are commoners, with no courtesy (consider their treatment of the old man), and un-Christian (consider the oaths they continually swear). They are dissolute gamblers and drunkards.

- **The quest** Conventionally, a quest would be to do a good deed, for example to slay a malicious monster that threatens ordinary people. The Pardoner's story is of a quest to slay Death itself, which is an absurdity. The tale gains its force because it is a subversion of all that is noble or honourable, and a parody of the kind of conventional knightly story such as that told by Chaucer's own Knight at the start of *The Canterbury Tales.*
- **The outcome** Conventionally, the noble knight succeeds in his quest and gains honour and fortune from doing so. The rioters ironically achieve their quest too, but this inevitably means their own deserved deaths. The audience feels no sympathy for them because of their evil natures.

Situational and verbal humour

'The Pardoner's Prologue and Tale' is full of comic effects. A few examples are given below:

> **'I graunte, ywis,' quod he, 'but I moot thinke**
> **Upon som honest thing while that I drinke.'**   **(lines 41–42)**

The humour here lies in the tension between the words 'honest' and 'drinke', which do not naturally sit together — unless the audience subscribes to the idea of *in vino veritas*, and believe that the Pardoner's open confession of his tricks takes place because he is drunk. The Pardoner's story, however, is too well controlled for us to believe that this is the case. Chaucer does not say so, but some commentators have considered it likely that the Pardoner recounts the whole of his tale while sitting outside an inn. This would be particularly appropriate, given that much of his speech is about the perils of drunkenness.

> **Ther cam a privee theef men clepeth Deeth,**
> **That in this contree al the peple sleeth**   **(lines 389–90)**

This is beautifully worded by Chaucer. It is necessarily true that all people are slain by Death. The inn servant's personification is glibly accepted by the rioters.

> **And preyde him that he him wolde selle**
> **Som poison, that he mighte his rattes quelle**   **(lines 567–68)**

These lines suggest that the two elder rioters are rats — very apt considering their treacherous behaviour.

Top ten *quotation* ❯

Deeth shal be deed, if that they may him hente.   (line 424)

The humour here lies in the beautifully controlled contrast between the rash arrogance of the rioters — 'Deeth shal be deed' — and the deflating word 'if' that follows. 'If' they could capture Death they might slay him — but in fact Death will capture them.

Bawdiness

Chaucer is famous for the bawdy aspects of some of his tales, and is sometimes presented as if he were primarily a writer of bawdy comedy. In reality, such tales are in a minority in *The Canterbury Tales*, but are more immediately appealing to modern audiences than the stern moralising of 'The Tale of Melibee' and 'The Parson's Tale'. In 'The Pardoner's Tale', bawdy language is restricted to a single passage, which gives its coarseness greater force:

Top ten *quotation* ❯

> I wolde I hadde thy coillons in myn hond
> In stide of relikes or of seintuarie.
> Lat kutte hem of, I wol thee helpe hem carie;
> They shul be shrined in an hogges toord!   (lines 666–69)

These lines are richly comic because of their crudity, but they are thematic too. The Host condemns the Pardoner's false relics, and all false relics, by suggesting that the Pardoner's testicles would be worth just as much. Moreover, there is a clear reference back to line 693 of 'The General Prologue': 'I trowe he were a gelding or a mare.'

Task **26**

Find your own examples of the types of humour in the text, and prepare quotations that you can use in your own essays.

That comment was from Chaucer the pilgrim, and this indicates that the Pardoner's sexuality was a source of rude jokes for all the pilgrims. The suggestion there that he may already have been castrated raises the subtle implication that he may previously have fallen foul of a man like the Host, and perhaps for similar reasons. This can hardly be the first time that he has boasted about his skills. The Host's remark in this case becomes doubly cutting if the Pardoner has no testicles to lose.

Irony

Much of *The Canterbury Tales* is humorous, and Chaucer uses many types of comedy. However, 'The Pardoner's Prologue and Tale' is dominated by the use of irony. If you have studied 'The General Prologue' you should be well aware of the varieties of irony that Chaucer uses, some subtle and some blatant.

The complexity in 'The Pardoner's Prologue and Tale' is that while Chaucer uses irony to expose the corruption of the Pardoner, the Pardoner also uses it himself.

The Pardoner's use of irony

The Pardoner is deeply aware of the irony of his own vocation:

> **Thus kan I preche again that same vice**
> **Which that I use, and that is avarice.** (lines 141–42)

❮ Top ten *quotation*

Hence his deliberate selection of his only preaching theme:

> *Radix malorum est Cupiditas*
> *(The love of money is the root of all evil)* (line 48)

❮ Top ten *quotation*

He seems to take delight in preaching very precisely about the sin of avarice, when he knows that it is his own motivating force. Similarly, he revels in the irony of his own ability to make others genuinely repent, while he remains a confirmed sinner:

> **But though myself be gilty in that sinne,**
> **Yet kan I maken oother folk to twynne**
> **From avarice, and soore to repente.** (lines 143–45)

Additionally, he makes active use of irony in his preaching, when he condemns sinners amongst his congregation:

> **Swich folk shal have no power ne no grace**
> **To offren to my relikes in this place.** (lines 97–98)

He knows the irony of his message — if the relics have no effect, it is because the person seeking their aid has unconfessed sins that invalidate the offering. No insurance salesman could more neatly trap his customers in a web of words.

In the story he tells of the three rioters, the Pardoner makes active use of irony to make his points more striking and memorable. It is the wilful blindness of the rioters that is most harshly highlighted, as when they speak of seeking Death — 'Is it swich peril with him for to meete?' (line 407) — or when they find the gold — 'No lenger thanne after Deeth they soughte' (line 486). The fact that the money is Death leads to further ironies of which the rioters are unaware: 'This tresor hath Fortune unto us yiven' (line 493).

❮ Top ten *quotation*

This idea is repeated four lines later when the speaker refers to the coins/Death as 'so fair a grace' (line 497).

The depth of the rioters' self-deception is clear when they talk of removing the money by night in case they are seen:

> **Men wolde seyn that we were theves stronge,**
> **And for oure owene tresor doon us honge.** (lines 503–04)

A more subtle usage is when the rioter accuses the old man of being in league with Death:

> **For soothly thou art oon of his assent**
> **To sleen us yonge folk, thou false theef!**   **(lines 472–73)**

There has been no suggestion of such an alliance, but the old man promptly obliges by showing them the way to Death if they are determined.

The Pardoner's employment of irony is deepened by his willingness in turn to assign it to the old man, whose use of it is milder but still retains all its force. This starts when he replies to the rioters' abusive challenge about his age by gently claiming that nobody 'wolde chaunge his youthe for myn age' (line 438). By the time they leave him they have driven him to a more open use of irony, which they still refuse to understand:

Top ten **quotation** ❯

> **'Now, sires,' quod he, 'if that yow be so leef**
> **To finde Deeth, turne up this croked wey'**   **(lines 474–75)**

He is well aware, even if they are not, that the word Death is being used metaphorically.

Outside the story of the rioters, the Pardoner's irony once again reflects on his own behaviour:

> **Now, goode men, God foryeve yow youre trespas,**
> **And ware yow fro the sinne of avarice!**
> **Myn hooly pardoun may yow alle warice,**
> **So that ye offre nobles or sterlinges**   **(lines 618–21)**

The only time his control of irony breaks down is at the very end. He hopes to persuade ironically the pilgrims to buy his wares even after he has confessed their falsehood. The Host's ability to see straight through the irony and trickery is a major blow to the Pardoner's self-esteem and beliefs.

Chaucer's use of irony against the Pardoner

Top ten **quotation** ❯

The ironies to which the Pardoner himself is subject are seen also to be direct comments from Chaucer: *'Radix malorum est Cupiditas'* (line 48).

That, if we like, is Chaucer's own theme throughout his portrayal of the Pardoner. He is exposing the corruption and evil caused by a man's obsession with personal gain, the corruption that has caused this loathsome man to subvert the functions of the Church and to sacrifice his immortal soul for the sake of short-term worldly wealth. His very profession is profoundly ironic — the man most in need of Christ's pardon is the Pardoner himself, but he does not seek it.

The corruption of pardoners was widely recognised in the fourteenth century, and Chaucer's educated audience would have been alert for signs that this one was wicked. Chaucer's portrayal can therefore be an uncompromising attack on the character and the way he preys on less sophisticated people. There is savage irony when he has the Pardoner say:

> That no man be so boold, ne preest ne clerk,
> Me to destourbe of Cristes hooly werk.   **(lines 53–54)**

It is not 'Cristes hooly werk', and doubtless any true priest or cleric would wish to stop him offering false hopes and false salvation. The Pardoner's expertise is a source of dismay for Chaucer:

> Mine handes and my tonge goon so yerne
> That it is joye to se my bisynesse.   **(lines 112–13)**

It is despicable to see such talents used to such false ends. We need to remember that the Pardoner is careless of others' souls provided that he makes monetary gain. Every time that the Pardoner condemns sin, the audience is aware that he condemns himself:

> But certes, he that haunteth swiche delices
> Is deed, whil that he liveth in tho vices.   **(lines 261–62)**

❮ Top ten *quotation*

In addition to his avarice, the audience has not forgotten that the Pardoner refuses to tell a story without a drink first (lines 35–36). The tale of the rioters, of course, gains extra resonance from the fact that their obsession with gold mirrors the Pardoner's own.

Finally, Chaucer's greatest use of irony is reserved for the end of the tale. The Pardoner, the master manipulator and employer of irony, is brought crashing to earth through the greatest irony of all, his complete miscalculation about the Host's perspicacity. The simplicity and directness of the description of the Pardoner's discomfiture — 'This Pardoner answerde nat a word' (line 670) — provides the culmination of all the ironies present throughout 'The Pardoner's Prologue and Tale'. It is worth considering that Chaucer's condemnation of the Pardoner also highlights the corruption of the medieval church, which licensed or condoned pardoners.

Contexts

This section is designed to offer you an insight into the influence of some significant contexts in which 'The Pardoner's Prologue and Tale' was written and has been received. AO4 (see p. 83) requires demonstration of an understanding of the significance of contexts of reception. Such contextual material should, however, be used with caution. Reference to contexts is only valuable when it genuinely informs a reading of the text. Contextual material which is clumsily introduced or 'bolted on' to an argument will contribute very little.

Geoffrey Chaucer illustrated as a pilgrim on the Ellesmere manuscript.

Biographical context

Although nothing is known about Chaucer as a person, and almost nothing about his private life, he was a prominent figure in the second half of the fourteenth century, with associations and positions at court. He served under three kings, and was entrusted by Edward III with foreign journeys handling the king's secret affairs. The public aspects of his life are therefore well documented, and demonstrate that he would have had direct experience of nearly all the kinds of people he represents in *The Canterbury Tales*.

There are some uncertainties and some periods of Chaucer's life for which little is known, but the salient dates are outlined below. The

approximate dates for the composition of his literary works are also
given.

Key dates and works

c. **1340–45**	Geoffrey Chaucer born, son of a London wine merchant.
1357	Becomes a page in the household of the Countess of Ulster.
1360	Captured while serving in France; ransomed by Edward III.
1366	Journeys to Spain; marries Philippa Rouet around this time.
1367	Appointed Yeoman of the Chamber in the king's household.
1367–77	Journeys abroad on the king's business.
1369	Campaigns in France; appointed Esquire in the king's household.
Pre-1372	*The Book of the Duchess.*
1372–73	First journey to Italy.
1372–80	*The House of Fame.*
1374	Appointed Comptroller of Customs and Subsidy.
1377	Edward III dies; accession of Richard II.
1378	Second journey to Italy.
1380–86	*The Parliament of Fowls; Troilus and Criseyde; The Legend of Good Women.*
1385	Appointed Justice of the Peace for Kent.
1385–1400	*The Canterbury Tales.*
1386	Sits in Parliament as Knight of the Shire for Kent.
1389	Appointed Clerk to the King's Works.
1391	Appointed Subforester.
1394	Awarded extra grant for good service.
1399	Richard II deposed; accession of Henry IV.
	Previous grants confirmed by Henry IV.
1400	Dies on 25 October; buried in Westminster Abbey.

Taking it
Further

Explore Chaucer's life in
more detail and consider
how far his worldview
as expressed in *The
Canterbury Tales* was
affected by his background
and experiences.

Social context

The three estates model

Medieval society comprised three classes or estates: those who fought, those who prayed and those who laboured to sustain the first two groups. In principle, this was the basis of feudal society.

The first estate was the clergy, a large group that maintained the fabric of society through the service of God and the regulation of human affairs. The second estate was the nobility, who were few in number, and were landowners and professional soldiers. The third estate was the vast bulk of ordinary people, who were subject to the laws of both the other groups. In a primarily agrarian society, this group comprised mainly peasants who laboured on the land to create the food and wealth by which society was sustained. A person was born into either the second or third estate, and might enter the first (the clergy) through vocation or for a variety of other reasons, including a desire for security or advancement. Otherwise, people were expected to remain in the rank to which God had allocated them at birth.

In addition to being members of one of the three estates, medieval women were also placed in three categories: virgin, wife and widow. They tended to be thought of as inferior in consequence and importance to men.

In practice, the structure of medieval society was not as simple as the three estates model suggests, and by Chaucer's lifetime significant changes had taken place. From the start, there were inequalities in the third estate, which necessarily covered a vast range of occupations. With the passing of time people strove to better their conditions, and by the fourteenth century there were numerous distortions and anomalies within the system. The range of characters in *The Canterbury Tales* illustrates this. The only members of the nobility are the Knight and his son the Squire. The only true peasant is the Ploughman. There are several members of the clergy, but only three women. The remaining pilgrims all occupy a shifting middle ground; they are technically members of the third estate, but to equate the Man of Law — a wealthy, influential professional — with the Miller is clearly absurd. Although class distinctions continue to exist to this day, it is evident that the feudal division into classes had already lost much of its practical significance long before the end of the Middle Ages; *The Canterbury Tales* amply shows how there was a blurring of position, wealth and influence in this period.

> A person was born into either the second or third estate, and might enter the first

Historical context

The late fourteenth century was a time of great change, which makes *The Canterbury Tales* a valuable window onto an important period in English history.

The Black Death

The catalyst for change was the outbreak of the plague known as the Black Death. This swept through Europe and devastated England on several occasions in the fourteenth century, most radically in 1348–49, early in Chaucer's life. The exact figures are unknown, but estimates suggest that up to 40% of England's population died. The effects of this were colossal. Before the mid-fourteenth century, the population had been expanding, meaning that labour was plentiful and land use was intensive. Afterwards, labour became scarcer, but pressures on land decreased. Thousands of individual jobs and roles were lost. Inevitably, there was suddenly scope for enterprising people from all ranks of society to seek better conditions and better occupations.

The Peasants' Revolt

Social unrest was a likely outcome of social change, and it is not surprising that the uprising known as the Peasants' Revolt occurred in 1381. This rebellion was primarily triggered by increased taxation, and resulted in a march on the city of London and demands for the eradication of serfdom. The rebellion gained little of immediate consequence, but it offers an important insight into the way in which society was changing at a rapid pace. At the time, Chaucer was living above Aldgate, one of the six city gates of London, so he must have had an intimate awareness of the events that took place.

Language

Further changes were probably hastened by the upheaval following the outbreaks of plague. It was during Chaucer's lifetime that English re-emerged as the official language of court and the law, supplanting the Norman French that William the Conqueror had imposed and paving the way for the dominance of what would become Modern English in the

during Chaucer's lifetime…English re-emerged as the official language

nation and beyond. This is reflected in Chaucer's choice of English for all his major works; by comparison, his friend John Gower wrote three major works, one in English, one in French and one in Latin.

The Church

Although it remained a paramount power both in politics and in society, the Church was also subject to upheaval at this time. In 1378, one of the years in which Chaucer visited Italy, the Great Schism took place. This was a rift in the Church which resulted in the election of two popes — an unimaginable situation if one considers the hierarchical significance of the pope as the appointed representative of God on Earth. The Italians had elected Urban VI as pope, but the French, supported by their king, Charles V, appointed Clement VII, who set up his throne in Avignon. Like the Peasants' Revolt, the Great Schism led to further questioning of the authority of established powers, and a greater willingness on the part of ordinary people to press their own claims for rights and privileges.

In England the effects of the upheaval in the Church were particularly felt in the work of John Wycliffe (1328–84), a reformer who attacked papal authority and denounced the Great Schism as 'Antichrist itself'. He argued that every man had the right to examine the Bible for himself, and sponsored the first translation of the Bible into English. He also argued that the Church should be poor, as Christ had originally intended, so his views are of particular interest in relation to the Pardoner, who is wholly devoted to increasing his own wealth. Wycliffe was a major figure in the latter part of the fourteenth century, and his work led to the heretical movement known as Lollardy. It is debatable whether or not Chaucer had direct Lollard sympathies; certainly his writing, in particular in *The Canterbury Tales*, attacks abuses within the Church in a way which Wycliffe would have endorsed.

Taking it
Further

Prepare a presentation for your class or group about Lollardy, explaining how it may have influenced Chaucer and whether in your opinion 'The Pardoner's Prologue and Tale' could be seen as a product of Lollard sympathies.

Cultural context

Chaucer's place in English literature

It was John Dryden in the seventeenth century who labelled Chaucer 'the father of English poetry'. The modern reader may share this belief, because Chaucer is the earliest writer who is still widely known. His language is the most accessible, and the most 'modern', of all the medieval authors, and his emphasis on apparently realistic characters and themes seems modern too. He championed the use of the iambic pentameter and the rhyming couplet in much of his work, and this metre became the staple of English verse for the next 500 years. He was well known both in his own lifetime and after; many writers, including Shakespeare, were influenced by him and used his work as a source. The term 'father of English poetry' thus contains considerable truth, but it is also a distortion and conceals facts of which the student of Chaucer needs to be aware.

Chaucer died 600 years ago in 1400. *Beowulf*, the earliest known masterpiece in English, was composed around AD 700. By that reckoning, Chaucer lived more than half way through the chronological history of English literature and represents part of a continuing tradition rather than being the inventor of a new one.

It is easy to explain both the error contained in the popular view of Chaucer and his pre-eminence. First, there is the matter of language. *Beowulf* was composed in Anglo-Saxon (also known as Old English), and even Chaucer's great contemporaries, such as William Langland and the anonymous author of *Sir Gawain and the Green Knight*, were writing in a style that dated back nearly 1,000 years. This was the so-called 'alliterative style', in which alliteration and a flexible rhythm were used to give lines shape and structure. In contrast, Chaucer wrote in a newfangled style influenced by French and Italian, using a set metre (mainly iambic pentameter in *The Canterbury Tales*) and rhyming couplets. His language was that used in London, and since London was the capital of England it was inevitable that Chaucer's language would be that which has come to predominate, and is therefore most familiar to subsequent generations. Moreover, until Chaucer's day there was very little 'literature' at all, in the sense of material that was written down. In a largely illiterate society, most culture was communicated orally, and written versions (including *Beowulf* itself) are fortuitous historical accidents. Most writing was done in Latin, the language of the educated (which essentially meant monks), and it is only from Chaucer's time onwards that there is a strong tradition of literature written in English.

A man as widely read as Chaucer would be familiar with all the great historical writers known in his time, together with many contemporaries. In addition, Chaucer's foreign travels on the king's business would have brought him into direct contact with the works of great European writers such as Boccaccio and Petrarch. Boccaccio's *Decameron* became a direct model for *The Canterbury Tales*. Chaucer was heavily influenced by

Taking it ➤
Further

It is important to be aware that Chaucer was a European rather than just an English writer, so it is worth exploring the French and Italian influences on his writing. There is an excellent introductory article at http://special. lib.gla.ac.uk: type 'virtual exhibitions' in the search box, then 'Chaucer', then select 'Chaucer's influences'.

biblical and religious writings, and by French and Italian writers of his own and previous centuries. It is worth thinking of him as a European rather than as a primarily English writer.

Numerous influences and sources, both general and specific, have been identified, and you should consult the edition of your text to appreciate the wealth of material on which Chaucer draws.

Story collections

In the Middle Ages, storytelling was a common form of communal entertainment. Literacy was scarce, and tales were told and retold, handed down from storyteller to storyteller through generations and centuries. Originally, almost all stories would have been in verse as this made them easier to remember, but as the Middle Ages progressed an increasing number were written in prose. Traditional stories might be gathered together by a scribe, and gradually individual storytellers emerged who adapted material to their own designs and added to it. Collections of stories therefore became common, some of which were mere agglomerations of tales, and others unified and written by a single author. A few of these collections are still well known, the most familiar example being *The Thousand and One Nights*.

Contemporary examples

allegory extended metaphor that veils a moral, religious or political underlying meaning

Chaucer would have been influenced by two particular works. The anonymous *Gesta Romanorum* was an amorphous and disparate group of tales gathered in various forms over a long period, but united by a single guiding principle. The tales, many of them traditional or legendary, were viewed as **allegories**, that is to say literal narratives that could be given a parallel spiritual interpretation. Each tale is followed by an explanation offering a Christian reading of the text. For example, the classical tale of Atalanta, the swift runner who is beaten by a competitor who throws golden apples to distract her from the race, is seen as an allegory of the human soul being tempted by the devil. It is worth considering how far *The Canterbury Tales* can similarly be seen as a diverse group of stories unified by an underlying Christian message. The *Gesta Romanorum* is also a vital reminder that medieval literature could be complex, and that medieval audiences expected multiple and concealed meanings in a work of art.

The second work, which may be considered as an immediate model for Chaucer, is the *Decameron* by Giovanni Boccaccio. Chaucer travelled to Italy and may have met Boccaccio; it is certainly true that he knew the Italian poet's work and was probably trying to create an equivalent masterpiece in English. The framework of the *Decameron* is similar to that of *The Canterbury Tales*, in that 10 narrators are given the task of telling 10 stories each over the course of 10 days, making a neat 100 stories in all. Chaucer's scheme has 30 narrators telling four stories each, making a more substantial total of 120 tales. The fact that this scheme came nowhere near completion, and that Chaucer probably reduced the plan to a single tale for each teller, does not reduce the significance of the comparison.

Chaucer's friend John Gower also produced a story collection, suggesting the popularity of such works in the fourteenth century. Gower's *Confessio Amantis* (*Confession of the Lover*) is a moral work commenting on the seven deadly sins, the same theme as the sermon in 'The Parson's Tale'. Gower also used some of the same stories as Chaucer, notably the tale of Florent (also told by the Wife of Bath) and the tale of Constance ('The Man of Law's Tale').

The Canterbury Tales as a story collection

The difference between Chaucer's work and these other story collections is the dynamic link between the tellers and the tales. The *Gesta Romanorum* has no narrator at all; it is merely a collection of separate tales. Although there are ten separate narrators in the *Decameron*, there is no great significance in who tells which tale. In Chaucer's work, the match of tale and teller is frequently a crucial part of the overall meaning. The Knight, the most courtly figure on the pilgrimage, tells a suitably courtly tale. The Miller, the most vulgar of the pilgrims, tells the coarsest story. In the most sophisticated case, the Pardoner, who would be a profitable subject for modern psychoanalysis, introduces his tale by explaining the hypocritical success of his own sales techniques, and then proceeds to attempt to dupe his auditors in exactly the same way. As part of this he tells a devastatingly effective tale of avarice and justice, which is integrally linked to both his personality and his practices.

The Canterbury Tales is remarkable because it contains examples of all the kinds of story popular in the medieval period — courtly tales, sermons, saints' lives, **fabliaux**, animal fables — and different verse forms, as well as two tales in prose. This makes *The Canterbury Tales* one of the most diverse of all story collections, and the narrative device of the pilgrimage plays an important part in giving this mix cohesion.

It can be difficult to appreciate the significance of Chaucer's overall scheme, both because of the unfinished nature of *The Canterbury Tales*,

Taking it Further

It is both entertaining and instructive to look at the *Gesta Romanorum* to see the kind of tradition that lies behind *The Canterbury Tales*. The *Gesta* were frequently translated into English; one version is available at http://quod. lib.umich.edu/c/cme. In Simple Searches, search for '*Gesta Romanorum*' and click on 'Early English Version of the *Gesta Romanorum*', then 'Table of Contents', then 'View'.

fabliaux short medieval tales in rhyme, of a coarsely comic and satirical nature

and because A-level students are usually restricted to studying a tale in isolation. It is strongly recommended that you acquaint yourself with *The Canterbury Tales* as a whole, perhaps by reading the complete work in Modern English.

Audience

Chaucer was a courtly writer, composing his works for a courtly and sophisticated audience. In earlier eras, almost all culture would have been oral and communal, with storytellers and poets reciting their works to diverse groups of listeners. The only 'books' were manuscripts that were copied by hand onto parchment made from animal skins, and these would have been rare and valuable. Almost all manuscripts were of religious texts, and it was not until the later Middle Ages that manuscripts of secular works like Chaucer's became available (more than 80 copies of *The Canterbury Tales* survive). By Chaucer's time, there were sufficient numbers of educated people and manuscript copies to enable private reading parties where one person, for example a lady of the court, would read stories to small groups of friends. An individual might even read stories alone, but that would necessitate the availability of a manuscript, and leisure to peruse it.

Despite these developments, the main mode of communication was still the public performance. It is helpful to think of Chaucer's original audience listening to *The Canterbury Tales* rather than reading them. No doubt Chaucer read his work to groups at court on frequent occasions, and his audience was mixed, with members of different social groups and classes present. In this sense, Chaucer's situation would have been similar to that of Shakespeare, who had to construct dramas that would appeal to the widest possible taste and intellect. *The Canterbury Tales* includes plenty of entertaining moments to elicit the most superficial of responses, yet also contains subtle and sophisticated elements.

Another development was that Chaucer was identified by name as an author and was popular in his own lifetime. Before this, almost all art was anonymous — the work of art mattered, not its creator.

Purpose

This consideration of Chaucer's audience leads to the vexed question of Chaucer's intentions in composing *The Canterbury Tales*, a subject to which there is no definitive answer.

It is helpful to think of Chaucer's audience listening to *The Canterbury Tales*

Irony

Irony is the dominant tone throughout *The Canterbury Tales*, and this makes Chaucer's work elusive and his purpose difficult to define. Irony always depends on personal interpretation, but not all interpretations are equally justifiable or defensible, so be sure that yours are based on wide and careful reading.

An example will illustrate the need for thought. Consider lines 630–32 of 'The Pardoner's Tale':

> **And Jhesu Crist, that is oure soules leche,**
> **So graunte yow his pardoun to receive,**
> **For that is best; I wol yow nat deceive.**

An inattentive reader might note this as a conventional preacher's comment, and pass on. A more considered response is to examine the immediate context. The Pardoner has just completed his tale of the rioters and explained that it is an example of the stories he uses in his sermons. It seems that he is genuinely telling the pilgrims that Christ's pardon is what is truly needed — but this is the Pardoner, who is trying to sell his own indulgences. His claim that he will not deceive them is precisely false: deceiving them is exactly what he intends to do. He is trying to lull the pilgrims with a falsehood, so that he can then begin the 'hard sell' of offering them his own wares. Furthermore, the reader will recall that the Pardoner is the person most in need of Christ's mercy. Finally, it will be noted that the Pardoner's hypocrisy does not invalidate what he says; Christ's pardon truly is the best thing to which a sinner can aspire. All these aspects need to be considered, and a good A-level student will be able to handle the sophisticated response required.

Possible interpretations

Modern readers must make up their own minds as to what they are going to gain from studying Chaucer, and this is often a reflection of what they bring to their studies. You will probably find evidence for all the approaches suggested below, but it is up to you to decide what Chaucer has to offer, and how he is to be interpreted in the twenty-first century.

Entertainment

Chaucer's tales are entertaining, and some readers wish to look no further than that. John Carrington, in *Our Greatest Writers and their Major Works* (2003), says simply: 'Chaucer has no over-arching moral or philosophical intention', and that he 'is driven by a curiosity and sympathy for life that excludes the judgemental'.

Task 27

Discuss this section in relation to AO3, which requires you to analyse alternative interpretations of the text, and AO4, where you need to consider 'the significance and influence of the contexts in which literary texts are written and received'.

Social comment

Many readers find some degree of comment on the behaviour and manners of medieval society. This could be anything from wry observation to serious satire, for instance a satire on the three estates class system or a developed thesis on the nature of marriage.

Moral teaching

Chaucer himself, in the 'Retraction' included at the end of *The Canterbury Tales*, quotes from St Paul's comment in the New Testament that all literature contains a moral lesson.

Devotional literature

As a development of the previous point, readers may consider the Christian framework of *The Canterbury Tales* and the idea that it preaches specifically Christian doctrines. The vast majority of medieval literature is religious in this sense, for example the mystery plays, such as the Coventry and York cycles, are based on Bible stories. *The Canterbury Tales* finishes with 'The Parson's Tale', a sermon about the seven deadly sins, encouraging many to interpret the *Tales* as having a Christian message about behaviour and morality.

Allegory

Medieval people were familiar with allegory, in which a surface narrative contains one or more further parallel layers of meaning. Such ideas were familiar from Christ's parables in the Bible, and the whole Bible was interpreted allegorically in the Middle Ages. It is possible to see Chaucer as an allegorist in whole or part; Robert P. Miller, writing in the *Companion to Chaucer Studies* (1968), comments: 'Each pilgrim tells his tale from his own point of view, but this point of view is finally to be measured in the perspective afforded by the allegorical system.'

Literary context

The framework of *The Canterbury Tales*

'The General Prologue' introduces *The Canterbury Tales* and establishes the framework that will underpin the diverse collection of tales that follow. It is worth considering the *Tales* as a whole to see what Chaucer was trying to achieve. It is well known that Chaucer left the work unfinished when he died in 1400, and it has traditionally been assumed that we have only a fragmentary part of what he would eventually have written.

Chaucer's original plan, as revealed in 'The General Prologue', allowed for 30 pilgrims telling four tales each, making a total of 120 tales in all. However, only 24 tales exist, four of which are unfinished, and although as the *Tales* stand nearly every pilgrim tells a tale, they only tell one each.

Narrative device of the pilgrimage

The Canterbury Tales is based on two great defining structures: the story collection and the pilgrimage. The latter serves two purposes in the work. First, it is a narrative device, and second, it has a thematic function.

The role of pilgrimage in framing the narrative is simple but important. It gives Chaucer a basic plot — 30 pilgrims travel from London to Canterbury and back again — within which he can set out the multiple and varied narratives of his characters. It allows him to gather together a complete cross-section of the social hierarchy (excluding royalty, who would have travelled separately, and the very lowest serfs, who would not have been able to leave their work), in circumstances in which the characters can mingle on terms of near equality. This equality would have existed in terms of their journey and experiences, but crucially there is equality of opportunity. Every pilgrim gets the chance to tell a story, and every story receives the same attention, although what the pilgrims choose to do with their opportunities is another matter. The pilgrimage is also dynamic, so that circumstances on the journey can impinge on the storytelling framework, as happens when the pilgrims encounter a canon whose yeoman tells a tale of his own.

Thematic function of the pilgrimage

The second function of the pilgrimage in *The Canterbury Tales* is even more important. A pilgrimage has two aspects: it is a journey, but it is also a sacred journey. Both elements are crucial to an understanding of Chaucer's work.

Journeys

The image of the journey has always been central to human understanding. Life itself is conventionally seen as a journey from birth

Taking it
Further

Explore the importance of pilgrimage in the Middle Ages, and compare how far religious pilgrimage is still significant in the twenty-first century. There are useful articles at: http://courseweb.stthomas.edu/medieval/ (select 'Geoffrey Chaucer', then 'Pilgrimage and Pilgrims'); and at www.meccapilgrimage.com/.

to death, and so any physical journey can be viewed as an image of life, with the travellers gaining experience as they progress. A pilgrimage is a special kind of physical journey, where the goal is a holy or sacred place. The parallel with the journey of life gains an extra significance, because the pilgrimage's sacred purpose is the equivalent of the soul's journey through life towards God. The best-known form of pilgrimage in modern times is the Muslim pilgrimage to Mecca, a journey that every devout Muslim is supposed to undertake at least once.

Holy sites and shrines

In the Middle Ages, the pilgrimage was a common and popular activity and there were innumerable holy places to visit. The most holy site of all was Jerusalem, which the Wife of Bath visited three times, and Chaucer also mentions some of the other most famous ones, particularly Santiago de Compostela in Spain. In England, the shrine of Thomas Becket in Canterbury was the most popular destination following Becket's assassination in 1170, and it would remain so until it was destroyed by Henry VIII in the 1530s.

The importance of shrines lay in people's belief in the efficacy of saints and holy relics, as is evident from Chaucer's portrayal of the Pardoner. The Catholic Church taught that God could not be approached directly; it was therefore necessary to pray to those closest to him to intercede. Along with the Virgin Mary, with her unique position as the mother of Christ, the saints were thought to be endowed with special powers and influence. The relics of saints, particularly their bones, were held to have mystical, almost magical powers, and there were dozens of shrines associated with particular saints, each usually venerated for a specific quality.

Taking it *Further*

Explore the importance of Thomas Becket further by doing an internet search. You could also investigate whether there was a medieval shrine or well-known saint near where you live.

Travel

Pilgrimage therefore held an important place in medieval life, but it was also a way to travel. In an insecure world, there was safety in numbers as well as the pleasure of company. Some of Chaucer's pilgrims, such as the Guildsmen, would be delighted to have a knight as part of the group, because he could offer practical as well as symbolic protection. A woman like the Wife of Bath would be pleased that the Guildsmen themselves were there, among whom she might look for her sixth husband; it would also have been difficult for her as a woman to travel alone.

It has been said that medieval pilgrimages were the equivalent of modern package holidays, and there is some value in the analogy, at least if it is seen as indicating the impulse to travel and the willingness of diverse people to band together for convenience and economies of scale. The comparison falls down, however, when the purpose of travel is considered. Modern holidaymakers largely seek pleasure, and few travel with an overtly spiritual purpose. The reverse was true in the Middle Ages; although a few of Chaucer's pilgrims might have purely social or secular motives for the journey, most would have a greater or lesser degree of devotion, and all would have been aware of the sacred significance of their journey, even if they sometimes chose to ignore it.

Symbolism

Every character, every tale, and every word of *The Canterbury Tales* is contained within the symbolic framework of the pilgrimage, whether the individual characters are aware of it or not. When the Parson tells his tale of sin and repentance, the connection is obvious, but the symbolism of the pilgrimage is equally relevant when the Merchant is telling his tale of an ill-judged marriage, when the Miller and the Reeve are trading tales at each other's expense, or when the Pardoner tries to con his audience through the techniques that he has just exposed. Every one of these is measured against, and judged by, the sacred context in which their journey and their lives take place.

The seven deadly sins

One of the most common and enduring aspects of medieval religious imagery is its focus on the seven deadly sins, references to which are still found in modern times, long after direct belief in such a system has faded. Deadly (mortal) sins were ones which meant eternal damnation unless the sinner repented; lesser sins were (and are) known as venial sins. There is occasional variation in the list of deadly sins, but this is the most common and is given in the order in which they appear in 'The Parson's Tale': pride (Latin *superbia*), envy (*invidia*), anger (*ira*), sloth (*accidia*), avarice (desire for money) (*avaricia*), gluttony (greed) (*gula*), lust (lechery) (*luxuria*).

Pride is traditionally the chief of the sins because it incorporates all the others. It involves a false belief in one's own importance, and is the sin through which Lucifer fell and became Satan, and through which Adam and Eve fell, tempted to believe that they could be 'as gods'.

Attempts have sometimes been made to demonstrate that the whole scheme of *The Canterbury Tales* was intended to be an exposition on the seven deadly sins, based on the fact that 'The Parson's Tale', the culmination of *The Canterbury Tales*, is a sermon on this theme. This

Taking it
Further

Look at 'The Parson's Tale' and compare it with 'The Pardoner's Prologue and Tale'. The Parson is the most respected character on the pilgrimage, and his 'tale' is not a story at all; it is a long, serious prose sermon on the seven deadly sins and how they can be avoided.

is doubtful, because few of the tales seem to be focused on specific sins, but it cannot be disputed that 'The Pardoner's Prologue and Tale' is a masterly exposition on the theme of avarice. The whole effect of the story depends on the fact that the Pardoner is guilty of a mortal sin which he is supposedly preaching against.

The route to Canterbury

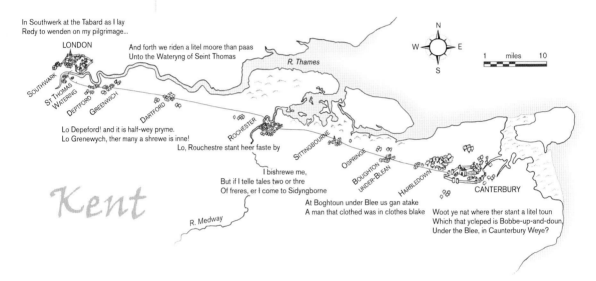

In Southwerk at the Tabard as I lay
Redy to wenden on my pilgrimage...

LONDON

And forth we riden a litel moore than paas
Unto the Wateryng of Seint Thomas

R. Thames

N
W — E
S

1   miles   10

SOUTHWARK
ST THOMAS WATERING
DEPTFORD
GREENWICH
DARTFORD

Lo Depeford! and it is half-wey pryme.
Lo Grenewych, ther many a shrewe is inne!

ROCHESTER

Lo, Rouchestre stant heer faste by

SITTINGBOURNE

OSPRINGE

BOUGHTON UNDER-BLEAN

HARBLEDOWN

CANTERBURY

Kent

I bishrewe me,
But if I telle tales two or thre
Of freres, er I come to Sidyngborne

At Boghtoun under Blee us gan atake
A man that clothed was in clothes blake

Woot ye nat where ther stant a litel toun
Which that ycleped is Bobbe-up-and-doun,
Under the Blee, in Caunterbury Weye?

R. Medway

The map shows the details of the pilgrimage in *The Canterbury Tales*, including the places mentioned by Chaucer in the text. The journey from London to Canterbury was nearly 60 miles long and would usually have taken several days in each direction.

The multiple narrator in the *Tales*

In a conventional novel, the action is mediated to the reader by a narrator:

Narrator

Audience

In *The Canterbury Tales*, Chaucer introduces further narrative levels that offer the opportunity for much greater subtlety. First, Chaucer the author introduces himself as a character or persona within the text, so that the situation is as follows:

Chaucer the author
▼
Chaucer the pilgrim
▼
Audience

This means that when you come across a remark in 'The General Prologue' like 'And I seyde his opinion was good', it is ostensibly made by Chaucer the pilgrim. The reader must decide how far it may also be Chaucer the author's view.

When it comes to the tales themselves, a further layer of complexity is added because each tale is told by one of the pilgrims, and reported by Chaucer the pilgrim. The narrative therefore reaches its audience at three removes from its author:

Chaucer the author
▼
Chaucer the pilgrim
▼
Pilgrim narrator
▼
Audience

Finally, when a character within one of the tales speaks a fifth narrative layer is added:

Chaucer the author
▼
Chaucer the pilgrim
▼
Pilgrim narrator
▼
Character
▼
Audience

The attentive reader must decide how far each of the narrating figures is in accord with what is being said. For example, the rioter in 'The Pardoner's Tale' asks rhetorically of Death:

Is it swich peril with him for to meete?   **(line 407)**

The reader needs to consider whether the rioter can so completely underestimate Death (he can, under the influence of drink), how far the Pardoner seems to share this arrogance (he knows he is a sinner, but shows no signs of repenting and thus faces eternal death), what

> each tale is told by one of the pilgrims, and reported by Chaucer the pilgrim

Find examples in 'The Pardoner's Prologue and Tale' where Chaucer and the Pardoner seem to be speaking with the same voice, and places where they are clearly at odds.

Chaucer the pilgrim's view would be (probable amusement at the rioter's naivety), and finally what Chaucer the author intends to convey about the nature of behaviour and pride in the context of the whole of 'The Pardoner's Prologue and Tale'. This last question is simultaneously the most important and, because of all the intervening narrative layers, the most concealed, and it is why critical debate about Chaucer is unending. In this case he presumably wants the audience to consider the rhetorical question both as it applies to the rioter in the story, and as it applies to the Pardoner in the context of *The Canterbury Tales*. A sophisticated reading is required. This is easier for the modern reader who has time to dwell over the text, where Chaucer's original audience would frequently only hear the tales read to them.

Chaucer the pilgrim as narrator

The subtlety in Chaucer's craft arises from the device of the pilgrim narrator. This persona is portrayed as a sociable but rather diffident character. When the time comes for him to tell his own tale the Host thinks he looks 'elvyssh' (otherworldly) and shy: 'For evere upon the ground I se thee stare' ('Prologue to Sir Thopas', line 697). Chaucer the pilgrim begins to tell a very poor story ('Sir Thopas'), but once interrupted by the Host he launches into a long, moral, prose narrative ('The Tale of Melibee'), which shows his erudition and seriousness. In 'The General Prologue', Chaucer the pilgrim frequently appears to be naive, most famously when he agrees with the Monk's low opinion of his own vows ('And I seyde his opinion was good', line 183). Often this encourages the other pilgrims to make further indiscreet confessions about their behaviour, such as the Monk revealing his obsession with hunting and riding. When he does wish to comment directly on a character, he can do so, as in the case of the Summoner: 'But wel I woot he lied right in dede' (line 661).

Critical context

All literary texts are subject to revaluation with the passage of time, and critical approaches will vary according to the concerns and preoccupations that apply in the critic's period. Each student, quite properly, evaluates the text for themselves. Your own considered opinion is what matters, but it should be based on the most detailed and measured analysis of which you are capable. 'The Pardoner's Prologue and Tale' is a fertile ground for varied critical approaches, because there is so much controversy about the nature of the Pardoner himself. As a result, it is possible to identify a range of critical stances that have been taken over time. It is up to you to decide the worth of each. The approaches below should each be considered and its validity discussed.

Historical criticism and new historicism

Historical critics tend to look at *The Canterbury Tales* as a product of its time, and look at it entirely within its original context. Some early critics even tried to find real-life counterparts of Chaucer's pilgrims, whereas others looked at Chaucer in terms of medieval literary schemes such as allegory, or the representation of what was called Estates Satire, examining the nature of society at the time. New historicists look further afield to the whole cultural background of texts, attempting to see how texts were formed by and reflected the historical, political, religious, economic and social circumstances within which they were written. In the case of the Pardoner, a great deal of attention has been paid to the role of pardoners in the medieval Church, and how far Chaucer's portrayal is based on genuine contemporary practice.

Psychoanalytic criticism

The apparent roundness of the Pardoner's character makes him an obvious candidate for psychoanalytical criticism, which attempts to subject literary characters to the same kind of analysis as would be applied to real human beings. It is easy to dismiss this approach, because a literary construct is exactly that — an artificial construct produced by an author for a particular purpose. In the Middle Ages this was certainly true — characters were often severely limited in scope, perhaps metaphorically or allegorically representing a single characteristic or idea.

However, a psychoanalytical approach can promote valuable insights if caution is exercised, and this is especially true of the Pardoner. His confession and his exposure of his methods require explanation, and an approach that concentrates on his possible state of mind seems quite natural to a twenty-first-century reader. The Pardoner can be seen as deluded, or as compensating for his sexual inadequacy by boasting of his other powers. He could even be seen as mildly schizophrenic, when he tries to make the pilgrims buy his wares at the end, as if he is unaware that he has previously confessed to being a fraud. Nonetheless,

The Pardoner can be seen as deluded

a psychoanalytical approach offers a very modern way of looking at a very medieval work, and discretion should be exercised in evaluating its worth.

Marxist criticism

Marxist critics look for what literary texts have to say about the power relations between various classes or economic groups within society. Chaucer's work is a rich source of material because it appears to be written at a time when many of the traditional models of interrelationship, particularly the concepts embodied in feudalism, were breaking down, and society was metamorphosing into something more recognisably modern. The Church too was constantly threatened by internal feuding, which would lead a century later to the Reformation.

Marxist political philosophy sees established religion as essentially repressive, and this would clearly be true in the case of the medieval Church. The Pardoner in one sense represents this oppression, playing on people's fears to extort money from them. However, the Pardoner is himself exploiting the power of the Church, because he uses its cover for his personal gain. In this way he can be seen to be manipulating the power relationship between the individual and the Church in his own interest, and might be viewed less harshly in this light than when considered solely as a moral agent.

Dramatic theory

This approach to literature entails looking at the text within its context, in this case *The Canterbury Tales*, and examining the way that the parts are built up to form a dramatic whole. In the case of 'The Pardoner's Prologue and Tale', this approach can be used in two ways. It is possible to look at the Pardoner in relation to the other pilgrims, and his tale in relation to other tales. There is clearly a 'dramatic' tension between him and the Wife of Bath for example. They are the two characters given extended prologues by Chaucer, and her extreme sexuality is contrasted by the Pardoner's lack of it. He interrupts the Wife's prologue, and receives a sharp rebuke from her.

There is...a 'dramatic' tension between him [The Pardoner] and the Wife of Bath

Equally, it is possible to examine the dramatic elements with 'The Pardoner's Prologue and Tale' — there is a range of voices at work, from the Pardoner and the Host to the characters within the tale, each offering a different perspective on the nature of experience and ways of living. The use of dialogue and setting is also comparable to theatre. There is an arching dramatic form reaching from the interaction of the Pardoner and the Host in the Introduction to their final explosive confrontation at the end of 'The Pardoner's Tale'.

Deconstructionist criticism

This is probably the most difficult type of literary theory for the student to grasp easily because it challenges the idea that texts can offer 'true' meanings. The nature of language itself means that words can never say exactly what we intend them to mean. Deconstructionists frequently look at the gaps and ambiguities in the language of a text. For this reason every reading of a text can be challenged by a counter-reading, and meaning remains elusive or undefinable. In the case of the Pardoner this can lead to the stripping away of notions of character and characterisation to examine the uncertainties and ambiguities contained in the language Chaucer uses.

Feminist criticism

Feminist criticism, one of the more prominent of modern critical approaches, has little to say about the 'The Pardoner's Prologue and Tale' because it contains no female characters. The Church was hostile to women, the Pardoner inhabits a world dominated exclusively by men, and he is evidently a misogynist, as demonstrated by his interruption in 'The Wife of Bath's Prologue'. The rioters, the old man, the innkeeper and servant are all male. Ironically, it is the Pardoner himself whose sexuality is ambivalent, with the suggestions that he is either homosexual or a eunuch.

Taking it **Further**

All these critical approaches should be considered as you develop your own response to 'The Pardoner's Prologue and Tale', but you may want to explore further those approaches which seem to you to be most valid. Bear in mind all the time that you will be extending your ability to fulfil the demands of Assessment Objectives 3 and 4.

Working with the text

Meeting the Assessment Objectives

The four key English Literature Assessment Objectives (AOs) describe the different skills you need to show in order to get a good grade. Regardless of what texts or what examination specification you are following, the AOs lie at the heart of your study of English literature at AS and A2; they let you know exactly what the examiners are looking for and provide a helpful framework for your literary studies.

The Assessment Objectives require you to:

- articulate creative, informed and relevant responses to literary texts, using appropriate terminology and concepts, and coherent, accurate written expression **(AO1)**
- demonstrate detailed critical understanding in analysing the ways in which structure, form and language shape meanings in literary texts **(AO2)**
- explore connections and comparisons between different literary texts, informed by interpretations of other readers **(AO3)**
- demonstrate understanding of the significance and influence of the contexts in which literary texts are written and received **(AO4)**

Try to bear in mind that the AOs are there to support rather than restrict you; do not look at them as encouraging a tick-box approach or a mechanistic, reductive way into the study of literature. Examination questions are written with the AOs in mind, so if you answer the questions clearly and carefully you should automatically hit the right targets. If you are devising your own questions for coursework, seek the help of your teacher to ensure that your essay title is carefully worded to liberate the required Assessment Objectives so that you can do your best.

Although the Assessment Objectives are common to all the exam boards, each specification varies enormously in the way it meets the requirements. The boards' websites provide useful information, including sections for students, past papers, sample papers and mark schemes.

AQA: **www.aqa.org.uk**

EDEXCEL: **www.edexcel.com**

OCR: **www.ocr.org.uk**

WJEC: **www.wjec.co.uk**

Remember, though, that your knowledge and understanding of the text still lie at the heart of A-level study, as they always have done. It is your informed personal response that will be judged and rewarded.

Working with AO1

AO1 focuses upon literary and critical insight, organisation of material and clarity of written communication. Examiners are looking for accurate spelling and grammar and clarity of thought and expression, so say what you want to say, and say it as clearly as you can. Aim for cohesion; your ideas should be presented coherently with an overall sense of a developing argument.

Think carefully about your introduction, because your opening paragraph not only sets the agenda for your response but provides the reader with a strong first impression of you — positive or negative. Try to use 'appropriate terminology' but do not hide behind fancy critical terms or complicated language you do not fully understand; 'feature-spotting' and merely listing literary terms is a classic banana skin all examiners are familiar with. Choose your references carefully; copying out great gobbets of a text learned by heart underlines your inability to select the choicest short quotation with which to clinch your argument. Regurgitating chunks of material printed on the examination paper without detailed critical analysis is — for obvious reasons — a waste of time; instead try to incorporate brief quotations into your own sentences, weaving them in seamlessly to illustrate your points and develop your argument. The hallmarks of a well-written essay — whether for coursework or in an exam — include a clear and coherent introduction that orientates the reader, a systematic and logical argument, aptly chosen and neatly embedded quotations and a conclusion which consolidates your case.

knowledge and understanding of the text still lie at the heart of A-level study

why does
Chaucer choose
the bipartite
structure of
confessional
prologue and
illustrative tale

Working with AO2

The key to gaining marks in AO2 is to be able to demonstrate how form, structure (how the text is organised, how its constituent parts connect with each other) and language 'shape meanings'. If 'form is meaning', what are the implications of Chaucer's decision to select this specific genre, and what are the implications of the fact that the Pardoner's contribution is just a small part of *The Canterbury Tales*? In terms of structure, in the case of the 'The Pardoner's Prologue and Tale', why does Chaucer choose the bipartite structure of confessional prologue and illustrative tale, and how do the two interact and support each other? In terms of language features, what is most striking about the diction of the text — monologue, dialogue, imagery or symbolism?

In order to discuss language in detail you will need to quote from the text — but the mere act of quoting is not enough to meet AO2. What is important is what you do with the quotation, how you analyse it and how it illuminates your argument. Moreover, since you will often need to make points about larger generic and organisational features of the text, being able to reference effectively is just as important as mastering the art of the embedded quotation.

Working with AO3

AO3 is a double Assessment Objective which asks you to 'explore connections and comparisons' between texts as well as showing your understanding of the views and interpretations of others. Clearly, access to the first part of AO3 will depend on whether you are studying 'The Pardoner's Prologue and Tale' as an exam text or for coursework. You will find it easier to make comparisons and connections between texts (of any kind) if you try to balance them as you write; remember also that connections and comparisons are not only about finding similarities — differences are just as interesting. Above all, consider how the comparison illuminates each text. It is not just a matter of finding the relationships and connections but of analysing what they show. When writing comparatively, use words and constructions that will help you to link your texts, such as 'whereas', 'on the other hand', 'while', 'in contrast', 'by comparison', 'as in', 'differently', 'similarly' and 'comparably'.

To access the second half of AO3 effectively, you need to measure your own interpretation of a text against those of your teacher and other students. By all means refer to named critics and quote from them if it seems appropriate, but the examiners are most interested in your informed personal and creative response. If your teacher takes a particular critical line, be prepared to challenge and question it; there is nothing more dispiriting for an examiner than to read a set of scripts from one centre which all say exactly the same thing. Top candidates produce fresh personal responses rather than merely regurgitating the ideas of others, however famous or insightful their interpretations may be.

Of course your interpretation will only be convincing if it is supported by clear reference to the text, and you will only be able to evaluate other readers' ideas if you test them against the evidence of the text itself. Worthwhile AO3 means more than quoting someone else's point of view and saying you agree, although it can be very helpful to use critical views if they push forward an argument of your own and you can offer relevant textual support. Look for other ways of reading texts — from a Marxist, feminist, new historicist, post-structuralist, psychoanalytic, dominant or oppositional point of view — which are more creative and original than merely copying out the ideas of one person. Try to show an awareness of multiple readings with regard to your chosen text and an understanding that the meaning of a text is dependent as much upon what the reader brings to it as what the writer left there. Using modal verb phrases such as 'may be seen as', 'might be interpreted as' or 'could be represented as' implies that you are aware that different readers interpret texts in different ways at different times. The key word here is plurality; there is no single meaning, no right answer, and you need to evaluate a range of other ways of making textual meanings as you work towards your own.

Working with AO4

AO4, with its emphasis on the 'significance and influence' of the 'contexts in which literary texts are written and received', might at first seem less deeply rooted in the text itself but in fact you are considering and evaluating here the relationship between the text and its contexts. Note the word 'received': this refers to the way interpretation can be influenced by the specific contexts within which the reader is operating; when you are studying a medieval text, there is a considerable gulf between its original contemporary context of production and the twenty-first century context in which you receive it.

To access AO4 successfully you need to think about how contexts of production, reception, literature, culture, biography, geography, society, history, genre and intertextuality can affect texts. This can sound daunting when you are studying an author as distant in time as

Chaucer, which is why this guide seeks to provide an insight into the contexts you need. Do not panic. Simply place the text at the heart of the web of contextual factors which you feel have had the most impact upon it; examiners want to see a sense of contextual alertness woven seamlessly into the fabric of your essay rather than a clumsy bolted-on rehash of a website or your old history notes. By being aware of the age in which Chaucer was writing, you will naturally convey your understanding of the fact that literary works contain embedded and encoded representations of the cultural, moral, religious, racial and political values of the society from which they emerged. Over time attitudes and ideas can change until the views they reflect are no longer widely shared. There is also significant overlap between a focus on interpretations (AO3) and a focus on contexts, so do not think about trying to pigeonhole the AOs.

One of the advantages of studying Chaucer's writing is that you cannot avoid talking about its contexts, both the ones in which it was originally received and how modern readers respond to it. It is always fruitful to compare medieval and modern attitudes and approaches, and sensible to recognise the different responses that might occur in any era. 'The Pardoner's Prologue and Tale' is popular because it seems to present us with a masterly analysis of a conman, a person who is simultaneously attractive and loathsome. The superficial realism has to be balanced against the deeper literary purpose that is served by *The Canterbury Tales*, and your task is to balance your interpretation of these elements. As Spearing puts it in the introduction to the Cambridge edition (pp. 22–23):

> **On the surface lie details so accurate that we can verify them from historical sources. But beneath them we find an 'unrealistic' literary convention, that of the confession. In real life people do not usually expound their own bad motives with the freedom that the Pardoner uses.**

Much will depend on the depth of your understanding of medieval art and its purposes, together with the modern standpoint from which you yourself approach the issues. Learn about the former by studying the *Contexts* section of this guide, and be honest and self-aware in examining the latter.

Comparative essays

The nature of the current A-level specifications means that you will usually be comparing 'The Pardoner's Prologue and Tale' with another

It is always fruitful to compare medieval and modern attitudes

text, whether in an examination or for coursework. Clearly much will depend on the text which you have chosen or are instructed to use in comparison, but you should ensure that you are fully familiar with both and have explored and understood all the areas where they can be profitably compared and/or contrasted.

Sample student essay

Although the following essay is solely about Chaucer, it is easy to see how the arguments in it could be developed for a comparative task. More sample essays are provided free on the website for the book at www.philipallan.co.uk/literatureguideonline.

Sample task

1 **What Gothic elements can you discover in 'The Pardoner's Prologue and Tale'?**

Student answer

Personally, I believe that the idea of the Gothic is best summed up in the words 'grisly' and 'macabre'. It is this which makes texts like *Frankenstein* and *Dracula* so iconic — the obsession with death and horrible violence. In this sense, 'The Pardoner's Tale' is a very successful Gothic text. 'The Pardoner's Prologue' is a rather different case, as I'll explain later.

At a superficial level 'The Pardoner's Tale' contains the basic Gothic elements. It centres on a quest for Death itself, and it features the grisly demise of the 'riotoures thre' who murder one another in hideous fashion, two of them dying with 'wonder signes of empoisoning'. Added to this there is the mysterious and macabre old man who desires 'an heyre clowt to wrappe in me', but who cannot die. Finally, there is the unchristian behaviour of the 'riotoures' who swear 'many a grisly ooth'. And I like the fact that to this character list Chaucer adds Death himself, 'that in this contree al the peple sleeth', and even the Devil, 'the feend, our enemy'.

The quest for Death is brilliantly presented, in my opinion, through the personification of Death as an active killer who 'with his spere he smoot his herte atwo' — the him being the rioters' friend, whose funeral ('a belle clinke biforn a cors') has already established aurally and visually the macabre tone of the story. The rioters instantly take up the personification and are grotesquely unconcerned about death: 'is it swich peril with him for to meete?' Their decision to 'sleen this false traitour' is simultaneously ridiculous and macabre. We may think the old man 'al forwrapped' is Death

himself, but Chaucer has an even more effective image in the shape of the 'florins fine of gold ycoined rounde'. We can all associate the lure of money with death, and so it proves to be. Although the rioters stop looking 'lenger thanne after Deeth', we know very well they have found him, and so it is. They immediately scheme against each other, the elder to 'rive him thurgh the sides tweye', and the youngest with poison 'so strong and violent'. These brutal methods of death are characteristically Gothic.

I think that Chaucer's particular achievement is to deepen the texture of the tale by adding a Gothic mood to these macabre elements. Right at the start the revellers 'doon the devel sacrifice' with 'superfluitee abhominable' — a phrase that could come straight out of *Frankenstein*. The Pardoner adds to the mood with his rhetorical exclamations — 'O glotonye, ful of cursednesse!' He does this again after the rioters' death — 'O cursed sinne of alle cursednesse!' — so the mood is kept constant throughout. The vocabulary of the tale is always set in terms of destruction and death, particularly when Chaucer describes the behaviour of the revellers: 'Oure blessed Lordes body they totere'.

Above all there is the character of the old man, who I think casts a sinister aura over the whole tale. He is the kind of mysterious figure who is common in Gothic literature. You cannot say exactly what he is supposed to represent — that is part of the mystery — but he is always ominous and evidently symbolic. He is like a *memento mori* in medieval art; he reminds us that we are always in the presence of death, a suitably Gothic theme. The rioters meet him 'as they wolde han troden over a stile', that is to say at a point of decision. It is inevitable that they will make the wrong one, particularly when 'this olde man ful meekly hem grette', and they, young and proud and 'al drunken in this rage', merely abuse him: 'why livestow so longe'? His tapping with his 'staf, bothe erly and late', is sinister, as is the fact that he knows where Death is, 'for in that grove I lafte him, by my fey'. Unexplained, inexplicable, he darkens the atmosphere of an already dark tale.

Top ten *quotation* 〉
Top ten *quotation* 〉

I have concentrated on the tale that the Pardoner tells because that is where the Gothic elements are concentrated, but in a wider sense the whole of 'The Pardoner's Prologue and Tale' stands as Chaucer's venture into the Gothic mode. 'The Pardoner's Tale' is set against the character of the Pardoner himself, and he is the kind of twisted, tormented spirit that we find again and again in true Gothic literature. He has the fascination of a snake, which is apt because he compares himself to one in his prologue:

'thus spitte I out my venym'. His very soul is distorted in my opinion, and he admits it, calling himself a 'ful vicious man'. The self-awareness of a doomed soul seems very modern: 'I preche of no thing but for coveitise'. I can sympathise with him to an extent, because he seems to be aware that he can do good to others even though he himself is evil: 'yet kan I maken oother folk to twynne from avarice'. However, he then repels any sympathy through his hardened attitude: 'I rekke never…though that hir soules goon a-blakeberied'. Like Frankenstein's monster, our sympathy for his circumstances is in tension with our horror at the evil that he does. The Pardoner is a real Gothic creation, and this adds another layer to the complexity of the tale he tells.

❮ Top ten *quotation*

❮ Top ten *quotation*

Overall, then, I believe that Chaucer has succeeded in creating a very Gothic text centuries ahead of his time. What this really means, of course, is that Gothic writers like Shelley and Stoker were picking up on the grisly and macabre elements that make medieval texts like 'The Pardoner's Prologue and Tale' so striking and successful.

Examiner's comments

AO1 — quality of writing
- Sound use of appropriate terminology.
- Assured knowledge of the text.
- Lucidly written and structured, with some striking and succinct phrasing at times.
- Assured personal voice and sense of informed response.

AO2 — form, structure and language
- Effective analysis of form, structure and technique.
- Very good use of apt and embedded quotations to support points.

AO3 — different interpretations
- Effective comparisons and connections (although this is not an overtly comparative essay) with Gothic literature in general.
- Lacks much sense of other readers' viewpoints.

AO4 — contexts
- Very strong sense of both the medieval context ('*memento mori*') and the true Gothic context of later centuries.

Overall
The student does best in AO2 and AO1, with clear appreciation of AO4. AO3 is weaker here, but would presumably be stronger if the task were

Task **29**
Examine the sample student essay in the light of the examiner's comments and consider how effective the essay is. What changes or additions would be needed to improve its grade?

Task **30**
Use the same title to create a comparative essay with a suitable text that you are studying.

directly comparative. The quality of informed personal response suggests an A-grade candidate overall.

Transformative writing

If you are developing a creative response to a text, for example as a piece of coursework, you should still focus on the requirements of AO1, including the need for 'appropriate terminology and concepts'. For example, you might choose to present the Pardoner's real thoughts about his prologue and tale, and his attitude to the pilgrims. There are numerous ways of doing this, and you may choose to create a very 'modern' piece exploring a very medieval situation, but you should show awareness of the mindset of a medieval man even if your terminology is modern. You could even make a virtue of parading your knowledge of some of the medieval context, thereby hitting AO4 as well.

Task 31

Write the Host's account of his response to 'The Pardoner's Prologue and Tale'. Think carefully about the form of this: you could imagine him describing later to his wife the characters he has met on the pilgrimage. His comments on the Pardoner may be forthright, and you should capture this in his tone and language. You could record his thoughts in a daily diary, although as the Host would probably have been illiterate, the task is slightly artificial.

Task 32

Imagine the Pardoner as an 'agony uncle' who writes an advice column in a magazine for young people. He has received a letter from someone who is scared about her own avaricious nature. Write his article for the magazine.

Extended commentary

In every kind of essay you will need to demonstrate your ability to analyse the way in which authors use language and form to create and shape meaning. You should practise this by writing analyses of particular passages from the text. This will have the added benefit of encouraging you to explore the text further, and will generate ideas that you can utilise in any essay you write.

Commentary: lines 609–32

This rich passage is remarkable in its range of stylistic and linguistic devices, and for the changes in direction that the Pardoner uses in order to sway his audiences. Equally, it is complex because most of it, from line 609 until the first half of line 629, is both part of the Pardoner's address to the pilgrims and part of his sample sermon. Simultaneously, therefore, we are listening to the Pardoner preach a sermon, to the Pardoner reporting the words of that sermon to the pilgrims, and to Chaucer (the pilgrim) relating the whole story.

The first section, lines 609–17, is a rhetorical and impassioned peroration, a summing up of the key message of the Pardoner's sermon. He reiterates and condemns the vices that he has enumerated earlier on and exemplified in his story of the three rioters. Murder, sin, gluttony, pride, gambling and blasphemy are crowded together in a succession of exclamations, and the Pardoner then expands his condemnation to include everybody: 'Allas! mankinde' (line 614). This is a clever device because it ensures that every single person in his audiences is included in the category of the sinful, and therefore all of them will require the services which he proceeds to offer.

This offer is made in lines 618–29, starting with the flattering but ironic reference to 'goode men' in line 618 and shifting from the rhetorical voice to direct address. The audience are all sinners, proclaims the Pardoner, but he states that he — and by implication only he — can save them: 'Myn hooly pardoun may yow alle warice' (line 620). The emphasis on 'my' in this line is masterly; the Pardoner will later correctly state in line 631 that the pardon comes from Christ, not from human hands, but in the heat of the moment his claim to hold healing power in his own hands is designed to offer a seductive instant solution. He mentions the price, of course, but emphasises that his audience will 'offre' this (line 621) so that it seems their grace rather than his charge. He focuses on the women — presumably as he regards them as being more susceptible — and ends with a final salesman's flourish, offering them total absolution and freedom from sin, 'as clene and eek as cleer/ As ye were born' (line 628–29). His ringing confidence and assurance here is designed to sweep people forward before they have had time to consider the validity of his promises.

The audience — both the pilgrims and ourselves, one suspects — receives a jolt in the second half of line 629, when the Pardoner reminds us that this is all reported speech: 'And lo, sires, thus I preche' . His previous eloquence is emphasised by the realisation that we have been caught up in the report of a sermon, and are not the original audience. In another abrupt shift of tone, the Pardoner takes on an air of mock humility as he records that Christ is the true pardoner in lines 630–32.

His final phrase, 'I wol yow nat deceive' (line 632), is laden with appalling irony, and allows us to unpick Chaucer's intention. The Pardoner's absolute intention is to deceive his immediate audience, the pilgrims, to whom he will now offer his services in precisely the

> every single person in his audiences is included in the category of the sinful

way he has reported in his sermon. Chaucer, of course, intends that we should not be deceived. We have followed every awful twist of the Pardoner's self-confession, and will watch in amazement as he attempts to deceive the pilgrims even after having exposed every aspect of his own falsehood. Chaucer means us to be in no doubt here; the Pardoner is a monster, a self-deceiving and destructive operative who undermines every aspect of the Christian Church with his false claim to be able to offer absolution. There is a moment of suspense while we wonder whether Chaucer will permit this villain to get away with his breathtaking arrogance, before the wonderfully comic release of the Host's destruction of his credibility.

Top ten quotations

1

Radix malorum est Cupiditas.　　　　　　　　(line 48)

This quotation, 'the love of money is the root of all evil', from Paul's First Letter to Timothy in the Bible, is both the theme about which the Pardoner preaches and the entire basis on which Chaucer builds 'The Pardoner's Prologue and Tale'. The Pardoner has one aim: to show how he can hypocritically use this theme as the foundation for his sermons, designed entirely to gain money for himself. Chaucer's aims are different: in one way he wishes his audience to take the genuine moral point that worldly riches are evil; in another, he wishes to undermine and expose the Pardoner and the corrupt practices that he uses. A century later, Martin Luther's attack on the same corruption would begin the processes leading to the Reformation.

2

For myn entente is nat but for to winne,
And nothing for correccioun of sinne.
I rekke nevere, whan that they been beried,
Though that hir soules goon a-blakeberied.　　(lines 117–20)

It is the depth of the Pardoner's sinfulness that would have been most striking for a medieval audience. He says he cares nothing for the souls of others, despite the fact that his vocation is supposedly to lead them nearer salvation. However, he seems to care nothing for his own soul either, because he must know that everything he does leads him to his own damnation. A modern audience will probably not have the same stark awareness of the choice between salvation and damnation, but the hypocrisy and brutal shamelessness of the Pardoner is still shocking, particularly when couched in the homely metaphor of the last line.

**Thus kan I preche again that same vice
Which that I use, and that is avarice.** (lines 141–42)

3

This is in every way a key quotation. The depth of the Pardoner's self-awareness is the most salient feature, and will provoke most debate about the nature of the character — is he psychopathic in a modern way, aware of his own evil and revelling in it, or is he cynically manipulative and dismissive of the moral aspect? Avarice, one of the seven deadly sins, is at the heart of the whole text and you must make up your own mind what the Pardoner represents here.

**For though myself be a ful vicious man,
A moral tale yet I yow telle kan** (lines 173–74)

4

This quotation sits alongside the previous one and the two should be learnt, and considered, together. The Pardoner admits to being 'vicious' — full of vice, sinful — and yet he is fully aware that his tale is deeply moral, and can act to make his audience repent. If his preaching encourages repentance, he seems to ask, does it matter if he is himself a sinner? You must make up your own mind, but the medieval answer would of course be yes. It does matter, because the state of his own soul should be the thing of most consequence to the Pardoner.

**But certes, he that haunteth swiche delices
Is deed, whil that he liveth in tho vices.** (lines 261–62)

5

This is a useful reminder of the importance of sin in a medieval Catholic context. A modern reader may regard vices as unimportant; they can be indulged or given up at will. To a medieval audience, however, sin was a matter of eternal life and death. The Pardoner is unequivocal, as any fire-and-brimstone preacher might be: if you persist in sin, you will be damned to eternal death. Repent while there is still time.

Deeth shal be deed, if that they may him hente. (line 424)

6

As so often, Chaucer's major effects are compressed into very concise phrases. The irony of the first part of the line is too obvious to need stressing; it is impossible to kill Death. The true power of the line lies in the tiny word 'if'. The rioters, as they make their oath, surely mean 'when' they find Death they will kill him; there is no doubt in their minds that their quest will be successful. The audience understands all the implications of the word actually used; you might be able to deal with Death if you could capture it, but you cannot. Death will capture you instead. There is a further religious perspective here, because only Christ can conquer Death, through his sacrifice and resurrection. The young men, blasphemous here as everywhere, seek to usurp Christ's role.

7

> And on the ground, which is my moodres gate,
> I knokke with my staf, bothe erly and late,
> And seye, "Leeve mooder, leet me in!"   (lines 443–45)

The enigmatic figure of the old man is beautifully caught in this image, along with a powerful reminder of the mortality that is the fate of us all, and particularly of the three rioters. The old man, desiring to die but unable to do so, sees Death like a mother, waiting patiently to receive her son. He is in powerful contrast to the three young men who desire to conquer death, and who will so soon be knocking at Death's door themselves, only to be admitted all too readily.

8

> 'Now, sires,' quod he, 'if that yow be so leef
> To finde Deeth, turne up this croked wey,
> For in that grove I lafte him, by my fey'   (lines 474–76)

This passage has a marvellous resonance. You can hear the scathing contempt in the old man's voice as he suggests that the rioters are blindly eager ('leef') to find Death. He points them up a 'croked wey', a phrase laden with significance. It is 'croked' in the sense that it bends away from the 'true' path that the young men should follow. It is 'croked' in the sense that it is evil, leading them to Death. It is ironic in that biblically the plain road leads to disaster, the narrow track leads to God, but here the path represents the temptation to leave the 'straight and narrow'. The old man's final line is similarly ambivalent. The rioters accept it as if it proves their assertion that he is in league with Death, interpreting it literally as they usually do. The old man's meaning is very different. What he has left is a heap of gold, which will represent Death to the young men. It has not meant Death for him, because the lure of worldly wealth has no power over him.

9

> No lenger thanne after Deeth they soughte   (line 486)

This is a perfect example of Chaucer's narrative economy and command of irony. The rioters have found Death; they are just too mired in sin to recognise it. The folly of their quest is magnified by their folly in failing to understand any of the signs and warnings they have been given.

10

> I wolde I hadde thy coillons in myn hond
> In stide of relikes or of seintuarie.
> Lat kutte hem of, I wol thee helpe hem carie;
> They shul be shrined in an hogges toord!   (lines 666–69)

All the Pardoner's swaggering arrogance, sustained through 600 lines of boasting, preaching and false moralising, is brought crashing to earth in this wonderfully coarse and graphic abuse from the Host. The Pardoner has dismissed the Host's intelligence and perspicuity; it is a delight therefore for the audience to see the Pardoner cut down to size by someone he has effectively been sneering at. The Host's insult is highly personal, mocking the Pardoner's lack of manhood and reminding the audience of Chaucer's hint that he is a eunuch. At the same time it is devastating about the Pardoner's profession, mocking the veneration of false relics. Instead of a saint's bones reverently enshrined in a glass case, the Host leaves us with the vivid image of the Pardoner's testicles buried in pigshit.

Taking it further

Chaucer's work

The standard edition is now *The Riverside Chaucer* (general editor, Larry D. Benson, Oxford University Press, 3rd edn, 2008).

Modernised versions: the best known modernisations are the verse renderings by Nevill Coghill (Penguin) and David Wright (Oxford World's Classics). While these give a flavour of Chaucer for the non-specialist, a prose version is more suitable for studying, because it allows direct comparison with the original text. The recommended work is David Wright's prose modernisation of *The Canterbury Tales* (Fontana, 1996). Although not currently in print, it can easily be acquired second-hand. It omits the 'Tale of Melibee' and 'The Parson's Tale', but is otherwise the best way to read the complete *Tales*.

Readings: the easiest way to hear Chaucer's work read aloud is via the internet; there are a number of sites that offer extracts or complete tales, and some give pronunciation guides too. See the section on internet resources below. Libraries may have audio CD versions.

Background reading

There is a daunting number of books on Chaucer available; your school and local library will have a selection. It is worth looking out for the following:

- Brewer, D. (1996) *Chaucer and His World*, Eyre Methuen. This is an excellent visual and biographical account of Chaucer. Derek Brewer has written and edited a number of accessible books on Chaucer.

- Burrow, J. (1982) *Medieval Writers and Their Work: Middle English Literature and its Background 1100–1500*, Oxford University Press. This study places Chaucer in his literary context.
- Gray, D. (ed.) (2003) *The Oxford Companion to Chaucer*, Oxford University Press. This major volume amounts to a complete encyclopedia of Chaucer and contains over 2,000 entries.
- Rowland, B. (ed.) (1979) *Companion to Chaucer Studies*, Oxford University Press. This contains useful essays on allegory and irony, and other essays on Chaucer and his background.

The internet

- **www.unc.edu/depts/chaucer/** is the 'Chaucer Metapage' and should be the first port of call. It is designed to act as a guide to Chaucer resources on the internet.
- **www.kankedort.net/** contains 'The Electronic Canterbury Tales' and a wealth of other information.
- **www.mathomtrove.org/canterbury/links.htm** is an excellent page of links to material on Chaucer and on the medieval background.
- **www.courses.fas.harvard.edu/~chaucer/index.html** includes an interactive guide to Chaucer's pronunciation, grammar and vocabulary, and interlinear modernisations of some of the tales.
- **http://englishcomplit.unc.edu/chaucer/zatta/Zatta_Index.htm** is Jane Zatta's site for *The Canterbury Tales*. There is first-rate material on the Pardoner at **http://englishcomplit.unc.edu/chaucer/zatta/pardoner.htm**.
- **www.fordham.edu/halsall/sbook.html** is the home of the 'Internet Medieval Sourcebook'. This is a huge resource of medieval sources and texts, including for example information on pilgrimages, saints and relics.
- **www.librarius.com/cantlink/pardonlk.htm** has useful further resources, information and essays.
- **http://www.luminarium.org/medlit/chaucessays.htm** has links to a range of essays about the Pardoner.
- **http://www.illinoismedieval.org/ems/VOL3/hicks.html** has an essay entitled 'Chaucer's Inversion of Augustinian Rhetoric in the Pardoner's Prologue and Tale' by James E. Hicks.
- **www.stjohns-chs.org/english/Medieval/pdr.html** gives a link to the text of G. L. Kittredge's seminal 1893 essay on the Pardoner, which is still worth consideration although much of its argument has been superseded in later criticism.